REAPING WIND

A MONTAGUE & STRONG DETECTIVE AGENCY NOVEL

ORLANDO SANCHEZ

Published by: Bitten Peaches Publishing

Cover Art: Deranged Doctor Design www.derangeddoctordesign.com

DESCRIPTION

You reap what you sow, and when you sow death...vengeance comes to collect.

The Dark Council threatens everything Simon holds dear. They want to erase Monty, kill Peaches and remove Simon's immortality—permanently. When Michiko goes missing, Simon realizes there is more at stake than he realizes. When Ken, Michiko's brother asks the Montague & Strong Detective Agency to find her. They must act, before the Dark Council implodes in violence.

There's only one slight problem...a renegade group of Blood Hunters blames Michiko for the loss of their weapons, one of which is bonded to Simon. They want the blades...and they want revenge.

Now, Monty & Simon must travel to Japan, find Michiko and stop the Blood Hunters before they eliminate an ancient vampire, without becoming the next target!

Will they find Michiko in time? Will they stop the Blood Hunters?

Jump into the next Monty & Strong adventure to find out!

ONE

"They that sow the wind, shall reap the whirlwind."-Hosea 8:7

Michiko's brother was in a foul mood.

"Where is she?" I asked, staring at the angry vampire sitting in front of me. I was aware that even though Ken looked human, he wasn't. "As in, where is she—now."

"What do you mean, 'Where is she?'" he snapped. "You're the detective agency—detect."

I looked at Ken, and refrained from making one of my usual remarks. He was known for spontaneous violence when irked. He had left irked long ago, and had fully entered pissed off, as waves of barely controlled anger emanated from his side of the room.

Peaches rumbled a warning under the table.

Ken took a deep breath and let it out. His usual 'shades of black' ensemble was Armani, and leaned more toward the formal side. Tonight, it was a black shirt with red accents and matching tie. The black suit was finished with lightly polished Zegnas—

black, of course. All this rested under a black Loro Piana trench coat.

I guess he figured if he was going to be an unstoppable, efficient, scary-as-hell killing machine, why not dress well? I noticed some of his hair had gone gray, which was impressive considering vampires didn't usually age. The pressure of leadership and keeping the Dark Council from imploding must've been taking its toll. He smoothed the wrinkles from his coat, and placed his carefully manicured hands on the table. In my experience, a vampire's fastidiousness was only exceeded by mage's.

We sat in Ezra's basement, which was a barely known de facto neutral zone and meeting area in the city. It was used when supernatural heavy-hitters disagreed on something—usually the wiping out of all enemies—and needed to have a meeting of the minds without blowing everything to dust.

No one would dare attack Ezra, or move against his deli, unless they were looking to shorten their lifespan to 'immediately deceased.' It helped that Ezra, short for Azrael, was the angel of Death, with a capital D. I appreciated that he was low-key about his deathliness.

I glanced at the end of the table where Ezra sat. He wore a pair of half-moon glasses, and peered at me over the lenses. He was dressed in his regular white shirt with black vest, and black pants. His rune-covered yarmulke gave off a faint violet glow, and he rested his hand over a thick book as usual. It was easy to confuse him with an elderly scholar, and not the personification of Death.

The runes and defensive measures in Ezra's made the Randy Rump look like an open-air market. Everywhere I looked, I saw symbols, faintly glowing with a spectrum of colors. The energy in the room was palpable without being oppressive, a subtle reminder that enforced diplomacy.

Beneath the enormous conference table, Peaches was

currently reducing the amount of meat in the world, one chomp at a time. Ezra was one of the main reasons my hellhound puppy looked more like an industrial-sized kielbasa instead of a streamlined hellhound of destruction.

<The place is the best place in the world.>

<I'm noticing you're enjoying yourself. How about leaving some meat for later?>

<Why would I do that when I'm here now? This is why you are so skinny. You leave your food for later. Eat it now.>

I shook my head. Peaches: Zen Meat Master.

We were sitting in Ezra's because Monty was *magus non grata* in the city with the Dark Council, specifically with the DCE— Dark Council Enforcers. They wanted to have a brief and ultra-violent 'conversation' with him about what they thought was his descent into darkness.

I didn't currently have the Dark Council or any other enforcement agency after me, but I knew that would be short-lived. I worked with a perpetually angry mage and a hellhound with a bottomless stomach. It was only a matter of time, really.

"When we last spoke," I said, "it wasn't under the best of circumstances."

"Are you talking about the small war you two started downtown?" Ken asked. "The kill order she placed on your creature, or the erasure she requested for your angry mage?"

"All of the above?"

"The problem is this entropy thing you three have going," Ken said. "It's real, destructive, and aggravating my—and the Council's—lives."

"Entropy effect?" I asked. "Sounds contagious."—I glanced over at Monty.—"He's probably talking about you."

"Chaos is the law of the universe," Monty answered matter-of-factly. "Perhaps you can clarify?"

"Spoken like a mage," Ken said. "You two"—he pointed first at

Monty then at me—"are like a butterfly effect, except with massive destruction."

"He definitely means you," I said with a nod. "*Butterfly effect* sounds like that wiggling thing you do with your hands. I use bullets and blades...not butterflies."

Monty glared at me. "Rubbish. There is no such effect. And if there were, it would be called the Strong Peaches effect."

"I'm noticing the omission of a certain mage," I said, raising an eyebrow. "It really should be called the Montague Peaches effect."

"I thought you'd appreciate the recognition and inclusion of your creature."

"Oh, ha...ha," I said. "British humor...got it."

"Indeed. Not everyone can appreciate intelligent drollery."

"Drollery? Did you just make that up?"

"Of course not," Monty huffed. "I speak English, not American."

"Are you two done?" Ken asked, his voice laced with frustration. "We have a situation with the war you almost started."

"War?" I scoffed. "That was more like a skirmish. Are they still upset about that?"

"Still upset?" Ken asked as his anger level ratcheted up a few notches. I have that effect on people. "Strong, that was only two weeks ago."

"Huh, felt much longer," I said, shaking my head. "Time flies."

"The area is still runically unstable," Ken said, pinching the bridge of his nose. "Which reminds me, Ursula wants a word with the two—three of you."

"Bloody hell," Monty said under his breath. "Are you certain?"

"Ursula?" I asked, confused. "Ursula who?"

"How do you think the damage your agency causes gets repaired?" Ken asked. "Not even mages can fix the devastation left in your wake. The Council uses DAMNED."

"You use the damned? That sounds a little dark, even for the Council."

"I didn't say *the* damned," Ken started. "I said—"

"Also that sounds like it violates a ton of labor laws. Do the damned have a union? Undead and Damned Local One?"

Ken just stared at me. I saw him mentally stop himself from shredding me. It was an impressive display of restraint.

"Mage…your patience knows no bounds," he said after a brief pause. "In any case, I'll let the mage explain it to you. Do not miss that meeting."

"You want Monty to explain something to me—right. That should be fun," I said, shaking my head. "So, is the Council still hunting us?"

"The Dark Council doesn't forget—or forgive."

"That right there," I said, pointing a finger at Ken, "that attitude is the main cause of stress. They need to let it go."

"They will," Ken answered with a smile. "As soon as you're dead, along with your agency."

TWO

"None of that tells me where Chi is," I said. "All I need is a location."

"She marked you, Strong," Ken said, exasperated. "How can you be so dense?"

"It's a gift," I said. "Years of advanced snarkery, distilled to its essence."

"The mark represents the bond you have."

"Don't remind me," I said. "That was not consensual."

"Stop kidding yourself," Ken answered. "Of course it was."

"What are you talking about? I never—"

"Your blade," Monty said. "When you accepted Ebonsoul, you merged energies with your vampire."

"Merged energies?" I muttered. "That explains why the bond is so—"

"Complex," Monty finished. "The bond of the blade is connected to the energy you and your vampire shared."

"She never said *anything* to me—never explained that."

"Would you have understood, had she tried?" Monty asked. "Some knowledge is best—"

"That's just it, she didn't try," I said. "Half the time I barely understand what *you* explain—but at least you try to explain."

I turned to Ken. "So I'm marked. How does that help me?"

"The mark goes both ways. She marked you, but the energy flows between the two of you on a constant basis. It's how she knows where you are at all times. That means you can find her—if you shut up long enough to focus."

"At all times?"

"That bond between you and Michiko," Ken said, "actually protects you."

"And makes him a target," Monty added. "A high-profile one."

Ken looked from Monty to Peaches.

"He's a target because you three can't seem to go one day without massive destruction," Ken said. "Do I need to remind you that they're still rebuilding the area downtown?"

"That wasn't us," I answered. "That was Tartarsauce and your people—the Dark Council Enforcers. Can we say, *overkill?*"

"They only arrived on the scene because of a certain phone call someone made to the leader of the Dark Council," Ken snapped, glaring at me. Easily a two on the glare-o-meter. "Let me see if this sounds familiar: *He's lost his mind. I don't recognize him anymore.* Those were the words uttered by a certain immortal detective."

"If I had to hazard a guess," Monty said, glancing my way, "I'd think he means you."

"Got it, thanks," I said, looking at Ken. "I only made that call to deal with a *situation* your Council refused to see. Plus, the Council threatened my family. *No one* threatens my family—no one."

I returned the glare, pushing it up to three, with an extra dose of 'Eastwood squint' to give it the proper menace.

"What's wrong with your eyes?" Ken asked. "Why are you squinting—at night?"

"The Council acts like all we do is destroy the city," I said, ignoring his remark and letting the anger seep into my voice. "We've saved it a few times, too."

"Usually because you're the reason it's in danger in the first place."

"*I* don't have anyone after me," I said. "Your Council is blowing this out of proportion."

"You were involved in killing Anastasia," Ken said. "Weren't you?"

"Not just involved. I'm the one who ended her," I said, hardening my voice. "If I had to do it again—I would."

"Did you think the Blood Hunters were going to forget that?" Ken asked. "How do you think they plan on getting their blades back? Asking you nicely? They know you're bonded to it."

"Shit," I said, grabbing a mug and pouring some Deathwish Extreme into it. Ezra made Deathwish with extra death and added, in my estimation, fatal amounts of caffeine—creating Deathwish Extreme.

Fortunately, my *condition* prevented death by coffee. Ezra's blend was literally not for the weak of heart. He took Deathwish and launched it into the stratosphere of flavor. Only my flask of javambrosia surpassed it.

"You got that right," Ken said. "Copious amounts of it."

"Does that mean they're going after Grey Sneakers too?"

"You mean Grey Stryder—the Night Warden?"

"That's what I said," I answered with a smile. "Grey Schneider."

Ken shook his head. Any moment now, I expected him to shatter the table with a fist and storm out of Ezra's. Well, maybe not shatter—Ezra *was* sitting at the table, after all—but pound it forcefully enough to crack.

"The Warden's bond will be easier to break since he's not cursed alive. He does, however, have some dangerous associates."

"Starting with a certain lizard who keeps trying to corrupt my hellhound."

"In any case," Ken continued, ignoring me, "yes, he is a target, but you seem to be the priority after my sister."

"I'm feeling all warm and fuzzy. Why me?"

"I don't know if it's your association with Michiko, the bond you have with the blade, the fact that you killed their leader or, as is the case with many people you interact with, that they find you aggravating and just don't like you. It's hard to tell, really. All of those are valid reasons to end you."

It was my turn to glare.

"And the Council's official position?" Monty asked. "Do they still plan on erasure and extermination?"

"I thought we were good," I said. "Hades said we were okay with the Dark Council as long as we didn't explode anything."

"The Dark Council isn't going to argue with Hades. Officially, you've been given authorization to operate in the city."

"And unofficially?" Monty asked. "Do they plan to honor the agreement with Hades?"

Ken shook his head slowly. "They are going to hunt you into the ground," Ken answered. "Some blame the instability in the Council on you, mage. The others feel this detective agency is more of a threat than the dangers you face and cause."

"Wonderful," I said. "Maybe we can have a conversation. Help them see reason?"

"If by *conversation*, you mean they execute you and your creature, then erase the mage, then yes, they'll be willing to have this 'conversation' with you."

"His name is Peaches—not 'creature,'" I corrected with an edge. "Just like your name is Ken, not 'bloodsucking idiot.' One is a name, the other is what you are. Why is this so difficult for people to grasp?"

"When I gave you the sword," Ken said, ignoring me again, and looking at Monty, "it wasn't so you could pass it along. Especially not to a god."

"You preferred the Blood Hunters possessed it?" Monty asked.

"I'm sure the killing spree Esti and her Hunters would have engaged in would have thinned your ranks considerably."

"Blood Hunters," Ken spat. "They're the reason Michiko ghosted."

"When did they get back in the city?"

"What makes you think they ever left?" Ken asked. "They want the Blood Blades."

He glanced down at Ebonsoul resting in my thigh sheath. The pull to absorb it was stronger these days. I knew I was being stubborn, but I preferred it in a sheath, not floating inside me somewhere.

"Blood Blades?"

"I need to go," Ken said, "before I do something that may get me killed. Like pound your head into the table—repeatedly. Your mage can explain the Blood Blades."

"Your restraint is appreciated," Ezra said, looking up from his book at the end of the table. "Please use the exit to the rear."

"I came to inform you..." Ken began. "As long as Michiko is missing, you are in danger. My guess is that she went back to our home in Osaka. We have property there, and Black Blossom in Hokkaido, near the Ioso River, but she never liked Hokkaido. Said it was too remote and lonely."

"Osaka, Japan?"

Ken stared at me for a few seconds. I wondered if I had finally pushed him over the edge. Surprisingly, he kept it together, didn't tear me apart, and took a deep breath. Ezra was an excellent deterrent to violence.

"Yes, Strong," Ken answered with a sigh, getting to his feet and brushing off his perfectly clean coat. "The one in Japan. Go find her. Before the Dark Council rips itself apart."

"I'll find her," I said as he left Ezra's.

THREE

"How are we going to find her?" I asked Monty. "I don't care what he said about the mark. I've never been able to sense her."

"Are you certain you want to find her?" Monty answered. "She will most likely be upset with you."

"What if it were Roxanne?" I asked, catching him off-guard. "What if Roxanne wanted me gone and wanted to eliminate Peaches. Would you go after her?"

"Yes," Monty said, without hesitation. "If only to find out why."

I nodded. "Then you know why I have to do the same."

"I do," Monty said, with a brief nod of his own. "Perhaps we can be prudent about this, considering how many—"

"First, let me see if this 'mark locator' thing works."

I closed my eyes, focused, and felt for the connection I shared with Chi.

"Simon, no!" Monty yelled, but it was too late.

I released what little runic energy I controlled. The defenses in Ezra's basement kicked in immediately and with extreme prejudice. The pressure around me felt as though a huge hand had closed around me. I opened my eyes to find myself suspended several feet over my chair, and enveloped in violet light. Monty got up and Ezra placed a hand on his arm.

"Tristan, don't," Ezra said, shaking his head. "If you do anything with energy, you will be in a worse situation. Besides, he has a few moments before the pain begins."

"Excuse me?" I asked, feeling the pressure around me increase. "Did you say *pain*?"

"I did," Ezra answered, pushing up his glasses to get a better look at me. "How are you feeling?"

"Trapped?"

"You can still speak, that's good. It's going to get uncomfortable in there in a few minutes. Before you ask, no, I can't disable it."

"It's uncomfortable now," I answered, as my breathing became labored. "Are you sure you can't stop this?"

"I'm pretty sure, yes," Ezra answered, grabbing a mug and pouring himself some coffee. "Looks like you forgot about the defenses. This is your life in a nutshell: act first, think later—or in your case—never. Being immortal doesn't mean being a putz. Some situations require a gentle touch...finesse."

"Every...immortal I've encountered...has registered pretty high...in putzness," I managed. "Present company excluded, of course."

"Of course," Ezra said, raising his mug in my direction. "You may want to conserve your breath."

I was losing consciousness, but I wasn't losing my mind. Insulting Ezra was never a good idea.

"Have you met Simon?" Monty asked. "He's not exactly familiar with the concept of finesse."

I groaned in response. The defenses were cutting off my air supply.

"I get it," I said with a gasp. "Gentle touch...finesse. Can we stop the hug of death, now?"

Ezra shook his head again. "Actions have consequences," Ezra said, holding up a hand, palm up, before turning it over. "You need to learn this. Feel it in your bones."

One of my ribs cracked. I grunted in pain and nearly blacked out. Sweat poured down my face, as heat flushed my body, dealing with the damage.

Monty was about to gesture. I shook my head.

"Don't," I said through clenched teeth. "I've got a firsthand feeling these defenses are stronger than you."

Monty slowly turned to Ezra. "Release him."

"Can't," Ezra answered with a shrug. "I wasn't the one who trapped him."

"I beg your pardon?" Monty said, as my vision began tunneling in. "Whose defenses activated? These are clearly not mine."

Ezra pointed at me.

"This is his fault," Ezra said. "He knew about the defenses and chose to do something foolish and dangerous. Cause and effect."

"Is it going to kill him?" Monty asked, looking up at me. "He's looking a little blue around the gills."

"It's fifty-fifty," Ezra said, shaking his hand. "Depends on him."

"Depends on him?" Monty asked, incredulous. "These are your defenses. How can their effectiveness depend on the person they're acting upon?"

"Oh, I don't know," Ezra said, peering up at me. "They seem to be pretty effective from down here."

"It's killing him," Monty said, gesturing. "Enough of this farce."

Monty unleashed a barrage of runes, and the room exploded in light.

FOUR

I opened my eyes to someone wiping my face with a pastrami-scented wet towel. Hellhound breath punched me in the nose as I shoved Peaches' massive head away a few inches. I stood unsteadily, barely escaping another slobber bath. My body was still warm from dealing with the damage. I remembered Monty gesturing, and the room exploding in light and power.

<You must be feeling better. Frank says my saliva is home pathetic since it can heal you.>

<I think you mean homeopathic.>

<No, he said you were 'a pathetic excuse for a detective, who needs constant healing'. That's when he called my saliva home pathetic—because it heals you.>

Frank and I were going to have some words in the near future. Violent ones.

"What happened?" I asked, looking around. "Where's Monty?"

"Over here," Monty answered with a groan from across the room. "Bloody hell."

<Does the angry man need me to lick him?>

<Let's hold off on saliva first-aid for now. He sounds cranky.>

<He always sounds cranky. He should eat meat. Then he wouldn't be hungry all the time.>

<You make a good point. I'll tell him to change his diet, and stop eating so many leaves.>

<Meat is life.>

I looked around the table and saw Ezra still sitting at the end, undisturbed. Whatever had just occurred in the room hadn't even shifted the yarmulke on his head.

"Sit," Ezra said. "Now."

The menace emanating from those two words was enough to focus my attention laser sharp. Monty limped over as I took a chair at the other end of the table. If Ezra was going to go nuclear, I wanted to see it coming, even if I couldn't do anything to prevent it.

"Both of you are hopeless," Ezra started, glancing at Monty. "Are you looking to end your life?"

"Not intentionally, no," Monty answered. "There was no need to cause Simon's death."

"Oh? So you're an expert on death all of a sudden?"

"Well I—" Monty started, before thinking better of it and opting for silence. Smart move, considering who we were talking to. Monty had ventured into *terra incognita* without a map.

"We'll get to that in a moment," Ezra said, turning to me. "Do you think immortals can't die?"

"Isn't that kind of the point?" I asked, confused. "Immortals can't die. That's why they're called *immortals*."

"The chutzpah on this one," Ezra said, waving a hand. "That mouth is going to get you killed one day."

"I was just stating the obvious—"

"Eventually, everything dies, Simon. Everything."

Ezra's voice reverberated throughout the basement. I felt the waves of energy cascading from his end of the table. I realized the defenses didn't react because this was Ezra's passive energy, and it was off the charts.

The only time I had sensed anything approximating Ezra's level of energy, was when I faced a god—a pissed-off god. Even that experience paled in comparison. My stomach tied itself into knots, and Peaches whined under the table.

<Why are you making the meat man angry?>

<I'm not making him angry, trust me. He's just letting me see a little of his real self.>

<His real self doesn't make me feel good in my stomach. Maybe I should lick him?>

<Don't think that would work. His real self isn't making me feel good, either.>

Fear—real, visceral, gut-clenching, limbic-brain, flight-or-flight activating fear—filled the space. It grabbed me by the throat and slapped me across the face several times, just to get my attention. All I wanted to do was run out of Ezra's, screaming.

"It is a law of the universe," Monty said, calmly. "Entropy is the only constant."

Monty didn't appear like he needed to run out of the room, screaming in fear—probably, because he was the thing most beings feared when they encountered him. That, and I knew he had made peace with death long ago.

"This way of being you two have," Ezra said, pouring more coffee into his cup and dialing down the nimbus of fear, "will have serious ramifications if you continue down this path."

"Which path?" I asked. "We're the ones being hunted and blamed for everything."

"Everything is connected, Simon."

"If you give us Ken's butterfly effect theory, I will be ill," Monty said. "We make our choices. Our lives are not a factor of causality."

Ezra shook his head. "I will provide you safe passage off the continent," he said. "Once you arrive in Japan, you must fend for yourselves."

"Couldn't you provide us safe passage—everywhere?" I asked. "I mean, you're—"

"Having the power and ability doesn't mean I can, or should, use it all the time," Ezra answered. "I just explained it to you. Everything is connected. My use of power does not occur in a vacuum. With great power comes—"

"Are you really going to Uncle Ben us?"

"Seems like you would understand it better if I use simple concepts."

"It's understood," Monty said, getting up and dusting off his jacket. "We do appreciate your hospitality and advice, Azrael. We need to see Ursula."

"I think a visit to Ursula would solve your immediate travel needs and keep your presence hidden," Ezra said with a nod. "At least until you arrive at your destination."

"Can you provide us with a circle?" Monty asked, prudently avoiding any more casting. "A direct teleport"—Monty glanced at me—"will mitigate some of the unpleasant effects for Simon."

"Of course."

"Thank you," I said with a nod. "I'll try to do that whole 'thinking before acting thing' you mentioned earlier."

"The odds of that actually occurring are astronomical," Ezra said with a laugh. "But, never say never."

<Don't forget to thank Ezra.>

<I will.>

<Do not destroy his business. Thank him softly.>

Peaches rumbled, letting out a soft bark at the end. Micro-tremors rocked the table.

"You are welcome," Ezra said, rubbing Peaches behind the ears. "Your bowl will always be waiting for you here."

"We're ready," Monty said. "Thank you for facilitating this meeting."

Ezra nodded, and a circle formed on the other side of the room. It was different from the circles I was used to; this one pulsed with red symbols, and vaguely resembled an oblivion circle.

"That's a teleportation circle?" I asked, warily looking at the angry symbols around its circumference. "Where does it lead?"

Monty narrowed his eyes and examined the circle. After a few seconds, he nodded unconvincingly in my direction.

"Seems to be safe," Monty said, approaching it. "Don't forget to call your creature, Simon."

"It should lead you to the DAMNED headquarters," Ezra said, rubbing his chin. "Or"—he removed his glasses—"it may lead to the Dark Council headquarters. I forget which."

"You forget which?" I asked in disbelief. "The Dark Council is *hunting* us."

"I know," Ezra said. "I do hope I got the right one. Would be a shame if I acted without thinking."

"I get it," I said. "Another teaching moment. Let's go, Peaches."

"Simon, if you pay attention," Ezra said, right before I stepped into the circle, "you'll discover that *every* moment is a teaching moment."

"I'll keep that in mind as we rush headlong into obliteration," I said.

Even Death was more zen than me tonight. Peaches stepped into the circle, managing to do so without dislocating my hip. He sat next to Monty and me, giving Ezra another soft bark. This one didn't set off tremors, thankfully, even though I almost lost hearing in one ear.

"Of course," Ezra said. "You know how to call me."

"I really hope he got the right circle," I muttered. "Or this is going to be a short and painful teleport."

"Have a nice trip," Ezra said, opening his book. "We'll talk soon."

With a wave of his hand, the circle burst with red energy and we left Ezra's basement.

FIVE

We arrived in a darkened open-plan loft. Judging by the view outside the large window wall, we were downtown somewhere. At first, I thought we were standing in some kind of abandoned factory. Most of the furniture was steel, or some variation of it.

What threw me was the lack of an energy signature. Even null zones gave off some energy. Runes used to create the null effect, released a signature, but this place was sterile—a void.

I didn't understand why we were taking this detour. We had the Dark Council and Blood Hunters looking for us; speaking to some construction crew didn't register high on my 'let's do this before we're attacked' list.

The layout of the space was pretty simple; large living area dominated the center of the floor, with other areas situated around it like spokes on a wheel. I made out the kitchen, home office, training area, and a door I assumed led to a bathroom.

All the appliances were modern and state of the art. The furniture was sleek, minimal and sturdy. In one of the far corners, surrounded by subdued lighting and several shoji screens, I noticed a floating platform. It took me a few seconds before I realized it was a Ruijssenaars magnetic floating bed.

"This looks pretty cozy for a headquarters," I said, looking around in the dim light. "You think Ezra got the circle wrong? Maybe he sent us to some upscale furniture store? That bed alone is priced stratospherically high."

"Unlikely," Monty answered. "But you're right, this is not DAMNED, unless they've downsized their base of operations."

"I wonder if I could sit on the bed?" I asked Monty as I made my way over to the corner. "This doesn't look like any headquarters I've seen."

"That's because it's my home," a woman said in the darkness, "not DAMNED HQ. You have two seconds before—Tristan? Tristan Montague?"

"Hello, Ursula," Monty said, turning around slowly. "I understand you wanted to see us?"

"Initially, I wanted to pound you," Ursula answered. "But that moment has passed. I thought you were part of something else. I put in the meeting request weeks ago. You just got it?"

"The Dark Council has been...otherwise preoccupied, it seems."

"Typical bureaucratic red tape," she answered, "with a supernatural twist."

"So, you no longer want to meet?" I asked. "Because I heard something about the damned, and I have questions."

Ursula was a tall, heavyset woman with short black hair, and the physique to match any Olympic powerlifter. She wore a white tank top and jeans, and down the length of one arm, I noticed an intricate pattern of runes. She closed the door behind her with a resounding clunk.

Her presence commanded respect, probably due to the enormous, rune-covered hammer she hefted in one hand, which, after a tense moment, she dropped it on a side table, with a thud.

<She smells like the bear. Ask her if she's a butcher, too.>

<She smells like Jimmy the Butcher?>

<I just said that. Ask for the meat.>

<We just entered her home unannounced. She looks dangerous, and that hammer looks painful. How about we talk to her first?>

<After you talk to her, can you ask her for meat?>

Now I understood why all the furniture was made by U.S. Steel. That hammer would've crushed non-industrial furniture flat. Orange runes pulsed slowly on the hammer's surface and handle as she made her way to a bank of switches on one of the walls.

"I'd prefer not meeting in the middle of the night," Ursula said, turning on some of the lights. "What are you doing here?"

"I was just wondering the same thing," I said. "It's not like we can't talk to the magical construction crew at another time. You know, when Esti and her psycho Hunters aren't looking for us?"

"Deconstruction," Ursula corrected. "We don't do construction. That's the crew after we get done with the mess you two create."

"Deconstruction?" I asked. "What are you deconstructing?"

"We're Decons and Magical Nulls—Elite Division," Ursula answered. "DAMNED. We safeguard the city's nexus points, maintain the balance of runic energy to prevent destabilization, and remove any potentially lethal residual traces. Like entropy vortices."

"That was an emergency," Monty said. "We were facing—"

"Both times?" Ursula asked. "Seems like emergencies just follow the two of you around all the time."

"That explains the absence of an energy signature in here," I said, glancing over at Monty and trying to change the subject. "You're a...magical null, right?"

Magical nulls were beings immune to any kind of runic backlash. They could handle the most dangerous artifacts with no adverse effects. Most of the time, they were shifters of some sort. Monty explained that, in the past, nulls were used as artifact guardians. It also explained why Peaches said she smelled like a bear.

"Correct," she answered. "This is the part where you tell me how you managed to get past my defenses. Not even an Archmage can teleport in here. Explain."

"Ezra," Monty said. "He created the circle."

"I see," Ursula said, sitting on a stool near the kitchen counter. She extended a hand, and the hammer materialized next to her, on the counter. "Even I don't have strong enough defenses to stop him. Don't think anyone does."

"Why did you need to see us?" Monty asked. "If this is about downtown—"

"No, I know that was you three—Hades, Cerberus and Tartarus," she said. "Not to mention the DCE unleashing devastating amounts of energy. We're still cleaning that up."

"Then?"

"Someone or something, is systematically attacking and destroying nexus points in the city," Ursula said, grabbing a Guinness from the kitchen. "It's not your agency. I thought it was related to you, but it isn't. This is different."

"Do you need our help?" Monty asked. "I'm sure we can offer some assistance."

"No, thanks," Ursula said, raising her bottle. "I'm trying to solve this, not reduce the city to rubble. Your reputation is quite impressive—especially your hellhound, Peaches, is it?"

"Yes," I said, impressed. "How did you—?"

"I have an affinity for animals, especially the 'hard to kill' kind." She held out a hand, and Peaches padded over.

<Be nice. Do not bite her.>

<Can you ask for meat now? You talked to her.>

"I bet he's hungry," Ursula said. "One sec."

She stepped to her industrial-sized fridge and grabbed an enormous bratwurst nearly the size of my leg.

"You really don't have to—" I began, when she gave Peaches the sausage. "Thanks, really. You just made a friend for life. One who will eat you out of house and home, if you let him."

"The last hellhound I met wasn't friendly," she said. "I'm glad your Peaches is—even if he is ultra-destructive."

<Don't forget to say thank you.>

< I like the bear lady. Maybe she's a butcher too?>

I looked at the hammer again, as Peaches inhaled the bratwurst.

<I don't think so.>

"Do the Norse know you've borrowed Mjolnir?" I asked, still amazed by the hammer's materialization. Monty elbowed me in the ribs. "I'm just saying, they may be looking for it."

"This isn't Mjolnir," Ursula answered with a smile. "I can see the confusion, but Kirves belongs to Ukko."

"Curvy?" I asked. "Your hammer is named Curvy?"

"Do the Blood Hunters know you have one of their blood blades?" she said, pointing at Ebonsoul. "Why do you wear it in a sheath? You're bonded to it. You can carry it within you."

She tapped her chest.

"Not quite ready for that step," I said. "It feels off, somehow, when I do that."

"The longer you wait, the harder it will be to resist," she said, extending an arm. "I can help you, if you want."

The hammer on the counter transformed to silver mist and evaporated into her hand, exactly the same as Ebonsoul did when I carried it in me.

"I'll think about it, when I'm not being hunted."

Ursula nodded. "You told me the how, now tell me the why," she said. "Why are you here at this hour?"

"We need to leave the city," Monty said. "Tonight."

"There's the door," Ursula said, pointing at the front door. "Besides, you're a mage. Cast a circle—outside."

"That's not possible," Monty answered. "The moment I begin a cast—"

"You'll have everyone on you"—she glanced down at Peaches —"like a hellhound on sausage."

"That would be accurate," Monty said. "We need to leave the city without alerting anyone watching for my particular signature."

"After today, what I need is a hot shower and another one of these," Ursula said, holding up her bottle of Guinness. "How do I expedite your exit from my home?"

"Maybe this is when you tell her *where* we're going?" I muttered to Monty. "Before it becomes 'hammer time'?"

"We need to get to Japan. Specifically, Osaka," Monty said. "Can you access a nexus there?"

"Yes, even one that won't get traced, at least not for a few days," she said. "But it's going to cost you."

"If it's financial remuneration you're looking for," Monty said, "I'm sure we can—"

"Please, don't insult me," Ursula said, her expression darkening. "Have you seen my bed? Money is not the issue here. I've reconsidered your offer to help. When I find out whatever is disrupting the nexus points, I'll call you and you will answer. Deal?"

"In exchange for safe passage to Osaka, agreed," Monty said. "On my word as bond."

Ursula looked at me and I nodded. "What he said."

"Good. Maybe I can channel your destructive tendencies for the greater good," Ursula said. "Let me get the circle ready."

"Is this trip going to turn my insides out?"

"You don't seem to be suffering now," Ursula said, walking over to the training area on the other side of the space. "You'll want to stay back while I do this. This process can get dicey."

She materialized her hammer, uttered some words I couldn't understand, and placed it on the floor as she stepped back. A large green circle appeared in the center of her training area around the hammer.

Peaches growled and chuffed at Ursula. She nodded her head.

"Are you really a werebear?" I asked. "Peaches told me to ask."

"Sure he did," she said with a smile. "I'll answer that if you can prove you're really immortal."

"I think it's time for us to leave," I said, quickly.

"How long before the trip is detected?" Monty asked, stepping into the circle. "They will be using normal methods of detection."

"My method will give you three days before they know where you went," Ursula answered, absorbing her hammer again. "Use them well."

"We intend to," I said, and the world vanished in a green flash.

SIX

We arrived in Japan just before dawn.

"We have three days," Monty said, looking around. "Let's not squander them."

We stood in a large garden in the middle of a larger grassy area. Monty sat cross-legged, taking in a deep breath and focusing. I looked around. Off to my left, I saw an ancient, large, fortress-like building of some kind, surrounded by a high wall. On my right, I saw a sizable lake.

"Looks like we're in some kind of park, a pretty big one."

"Open land is scarce in Japan," Monty answered. "Large parks like this aren't overly common."

"Do you know where we are?" I asked, looking off into the distance. "None of this looks familiar to me."

"That structure looks like Osaka Castle, which would make this Osaka Castle Park."

"Makes sense," I said, taking in the sight. "What are you doing?"

"Attuning our energy signatures," Monty said, closing his eyes. "I'd like to avoid detection for as long as possible."

"Good plan," I answered. "A question, though."

"Can it wait?" Monty asked, without opening his eyes. "I'm trying to see if I can sense any trace energy signature of your vampire in the immediate area."

"That would help," I said. "Monty, do you remember when we arrived in London? When the Penumbra Consortium rolled out the welcome committee?"

"Yes," Monty said, keeping his eyes closed as his body floated a few inches above the ground, turning slowly. "I seem to recall it wasn't much of a welcome."

"Do you think every country has some variation of the Dark Council?"

"I would imagine so," Monty answered. "Why do you ask?"

"Seems like the attuning thing you're trying to do didn't work."

"If you would stop interrupting and let me start—"

"I thought you had begun. Your eyes were closed, and you looked very 'one with the Force,' attuned and all."

"One with the what?"

"Are you serious?" I asked. "Say it with me: 'I am one with the Force. The Force is with me.' Maybe it will speed up the process?"

"The process you keep interrupting?" Monty asked, keeping his eyes closed.

"Not my fault this attuning thing isn't working," I said. "How long do you think it will take?"

"I've barely started," Monty snapped. "Is there a point to the questioning?"

"Oh, no reason," I replied, as Peaches entered 'shred and rend' mode with a low growl. "It just looks like that group over there, with the drawn swords, wants to have a chat."

<Get ready to protect Monty, in case they attack.>

<Can I bite them?>

<Only if they attack. Bite them, but no ripping off arms or legs.>

<Frank says sometimes one good bite can be a detergent. It will stop the other bad people.>

<I think you mean deterrent. Detergent is used to clean things, like your clothes.>

<Do you use deterrent to clean your clothes?>

<No, I use—never mind. Just make sure they stay in one piece if they attack.>

<Okay, soft bites, but no ripping or chewing.>

<Let's start with being friendly before you chew on them.>

In the distance stood a group in a semicircle formation. The six men and one woman were dressed in formal business attire. When I looked closer, I noticed all of the men had drawn their swords. The woman in the center was empty-handed, arms crossed in front of her body. She was the one I kept my eyes on.

They looked like angry bankers, except most of the bankers I knew didn't wield softly glowing swords. They wore black suits, white shirts, and scowls. We were facing either bankers or mages —or possibly bankermages. The violet glow around the swords had me thinking the bankermages were about to execute our last transaction.

I had non-lethal, synapse-disrupting, persuader rounds in Grim Whisper. I thought the non-fatal approach would make a better first impression on foreign soil. Apparently, however they hadn't received the same memo the edges on those swords were definitely in the lethal category.

"What?" Monty said, opening his eyes, getting to his feet and brushing off his suit as he turned to our welcoming committee. "They look displeased."

"What gave you that impression?" I asked, opening my jacket to give me access to Grim Whisper. "The angry expressions or the glowing swords?"

"Both," Monty said. "Let's start this interaction with diplomacy, shall we?"

"Sure," I muttered under my breath as the group approached. "We've had a great track record with diplomacy. I thought Uhura said we had three days? We didn't do one of those Ziller time slides things, did we?"

"Not to my knowledge," Monty said, keeping his hands wiggle-free and in plain sight. "Her name is Ursula, by the way. Can you calm your creature down? Our hosts seem agitated as it is, and his 'smile' isn't helping."

"Do you want me to try and communicate with the bankermages?"

"Bankermages, really?" Monty asked. "I'm surprised you didn't go with renegade sushi chefs."

"That was my second guess, but I really wasn't getting the chef vibe from them."

"I'm fairly certain these aren't Blood Hunters," Monty replied, narrowing his eyes. "The attire and time of day are wrong."

"The glowing swords have me leaning toward mages, but the dress code is too corporate for regular mages. These guys are not shopping on High Street."

"Are you implying they are part-time mages?"

"Or part-time bankers," I answered, glancing at him. "I'm not sensing the level of anger I get from some mages. They seem upset, but it's not that seething undercurrent of rage most mages exhibit."

"I do not have a seething undercurrent of mage," Monty snapped, pulling on a sleeve. "Let's see how cheerful *you* are after a few centuries."

"Like I said, not getting that uber cranky vibe from them. They seem more along the lines of 'we will stab and slice you for offending us' angry."

"Then it's probably better if you don't approach them."

"Maybe they're just here to tell us to get off their lawn?" I said. "I could ask if they know where the Nakatomi residence is."

"I think you should let me do the talking," Monty answered. "We agreed on diplomacy first."

"Good idea," I said. "My Japanese is rusty. I'd probably

challenge them to a duel or call their mothers smelly pigs—which wouldn't be diplomatic at all."

"Your fluency with the language is not an issue," Monty said. "If I recall, your Japanese is serviceable. If you'd like, I can cast a babel rune?"

"Pass. There's always something lost in translation, even if the translation is magical."

A babel rune allowed anyone under its effect to understand any spoken language.

"Babel runes are extremely accurate," Monty said. "I doubt it will impede your ability to communicate."

"That's just for my understanding of what *they* are saying," I clarified. "I may still call them 'scruffy-looking nerfherders.'"

"I don't even want to know," Monty replied. "And for your information, the babel rune translates your speech as well, such that the listener can understand you."

"I wonder what 'nerfherder' sounds like in Japanese? Do you think it even translates?"

Monty shot me a glare, before walking ahead to meet the approaching mages. I turned to Peaches, who was beaming his best hellhound smile at the group. His smile hovered between full-on 'tear you to pieces' and 'going to chew on your bones' intensity.

<Hey boy, turn down the shredding stance, and stop smiling. Monty is going to talk to them.>

<You told me to be friendly. Smiles are friendly. Do you think they have meat?>

<Hellhound smiles aren't that friendly.>

<Do I need to practice my smile?>

<I don't think practice is going to help.>

<Just like practice doesn't help your magic?>

<I'm not a mage, and my magic is getting better.>

<I don't think so. Your meat tastes bad, and your magic is not very strong.>

<I'm working on it. Some of us aren't born awesome like hellhounds.>

<Can you ask? I'm hungry.>

<If they do, they don't look like the sharing type. Let's not make them angrier than they are. Monty is going to see if he can convince them to go home.>

I walked slowly behind Monty, giving him space to approach the cranky bankermage committee alone first. I had a few questions.

SEVEN

As we approached the group, I was certain the bankermages weren't vampire killers. They lacked a certain deranged blood lust I've come to associate with Blood Hunters. This group looked at us like we had entered their territory, and they were going to escort us out—in pieces, if needed.

The sun was creeping over the horizon, brightening the cloudless sky. Dawn was minutes away, and Blood Hunters did most of their work in the dead of night. Also, the fact that we weren't vampires factored heavily in my assessment. Still, they looked angry about something.

"Maybe we're standing in a sacred park or something?" I said as I stepped behind Monty. "How did they know we were going to show up here?"

"A good question," Monty said without turning. "If you give me a moment, I'll ask her."

I let my hand rest on Grim Whisper. If they were going to be holding drawn swords, I wanted to be ready if the conversation suddenly became bladed. Call me cynical, but I didn't trust angry mages holding glowing swords. Actually, outside of Monty and maybe Dex, I didn't trust mages much...period. The ones I knew were either borderline crazy, full-blown psychotic, or too powerful not to instill a healthy fear when around them.

It probably had something to do with manipulating that much energy, frying some of the important neurons. Another reason for me to stay away from magic and magic weapons. The six men hung back and let the woman step forward to meet Monty.

"Maybe she is going to politely inform you that we are trespassing and are about to be repeatedly stabbed and sliced. Japan *is* big on manners."

"Can you, for at least two minutes, exercise some restraint before speaking?" Monty asked, while remaining focused on the woman. "I'd prefer this not become an incident."

"I'm a master of restraint," I muttered. "Are you kidding? Watch me and my powers of restraint. As long as they refrain from going ginsu on us, restraint is my middle name."

Monty sighed and shook his head. He bowed when the woman stepped a little closer to us and stopped. She returned the bow, glancing at Peaches for a second before returning her gaze to Monty.

"*Ohayogozaimasu,* good morning," Monty said."I am—"

"Tristan Montague, mage of the Golden Circle," the woman finished in crisp English and turned to me. "You are Simon Strong, and that"—she pointed a finger at Peaches—"is your *tenma* dog."

She looked down at Peaches with an expression of disgust, which made my fingers twitchy. Her tone immediately set me on edge. I didn't need to understand the word to get the meaning behind it, but in the spirit of positive foreign relations and diplomacy, I would give her a chance to explain.

"*Tenma?*" I asked. "I'm sorry, my Japanese is rusty. Can you explain?"

The woman turned her expressionless face and looked at me.

"*Tenma* means monster, evil spirit, or demon," she said,

glancing at Peaches again. "Is this inaccurate? Your creature is a demon dog, and should be exterminated."

"Simon—" Monty said, warning me with his eyes. "It's quite possible something is lost in translation."

"For the record," I said quietly, "the fact that my gun is still holstered demonstrates my phenomenal restraint."

"Duly noted," Monty said. "Perhaps she really meant contained?"

"*Exterminated* sounded pretty clear to me," I said, letting the anger seep into my voice. "He is not a *tenma*, or monster. His name is Peaches, and if you touch him you are going to have a problem."

"*Momo?*" the woman replied. "Are you certain?"

"Momo? I didn't say his name is Momo, I said his name—"

"*Momo* is Japanese for peach, Simon," Monty said. "Let's find out who they are before we start shooting."

"I am Fumiko Ishikawa, Osaka Regional Director of *Kuro Hyogikai*, the Japanese Dark Council," she said. "You are to surrender to my authority or face the consequences."

EIGHT

"There must be some misunderstanding," Monty said, stepping back. "We have no quarrel with you or your country."

"Why would you have a quarrel with us?" Fumiko answered with a slight smile and made a subtle gesture. "You three are the ones responsible for the extensive damage recently inflicted on New York City."

I looked around for some kind of attack after her gesture, but nothing appeared.

"You feel anything weird after that hand motion?" I asked Monty under my breath. "I'm sensing something, but it reads off."

Monty nodded. "Stay alert," he replied. "She is stronger than she looks. She just cast some kind of disruption wave."

I saw the runes on Peaches' flanks turn golden as he gave off a low growl.

<Stay back. She's dangerous, boy.>
<She made my sides feel funny.>
<What do you mean? Funny?>
<It's gone now. It felt hot on my sides.>
<Are you okay? Do you feel bad?>

<No. Your meat made my insides feel bad. But she makes my sides feel warm.>

The runes on his sides pulsed gold for a few more seconds, then faded back to normal.

"We were not the ones responsible for the destruction in New York City," Monty said. "You have been misinformed."

"We were informed that you had gone dark," Fumiko answered. "There is evidence to suggest you've used blood magic and allied yourselves with Hades, as well as Cerberus, his hellhound"—she glanced at Peaches—"another monster."

"What evidence?" Monty asked in a clipped voice. I could tell he was getting upset. "I don't recall seeing you there."

"Hades entrusted his weapon, a bident, to you. Why would he do that?"

"To stop Tartarboy," I snapped. "Who, by the way, was going to destroy everything. Are you *not* listening?"

"And you felt the best way to prevent this was to obliterate lower Manhattan?"

"What did you do to Peaches?" I asked, suddenly angry that she wasn't even making an attempt to understand our explanation. "You did *something* to him."

"I took precautions," Fumiko answered. "I'm not going to let you or your monster destroy my city, like you did yours."

"That was the DCE," I said, letting my senses expand. "We were trying to prevent Tartarsauce from destroying everything."

"And in the process, nearly started a war?" Fumiko asked. "You have an interesting way of saving your city."

"You had to be there," I said, realizing Monty was gathering energy. "If we hadn't stopped Tartarsauce—"

"By using the Dark Council as your personal army."

"The city would be dust right now," I finished. "Then they try and blame the damage on us?"

"I see," Fumiko said with a nod. "And I'm certain the

Penumbra Consortium was mistaken when they detailed the amount of damage your visit incurred on the city of London?"

"There were...extenuating circumstances," I said, glancing at Monty. "If the Consortium—"

"Starting with the destruction of the TATE Modern, which I am informed was caused by that creature?" Fumiko interrupted. "It appears that everywhere you go, chaos and destruction follow you."

"Seems like the Dark Council informed everyone," I said. "Did they explain the circumstances?"

"Every global branch of the Dark Council has been informed of the *Trio* of Terror," Fumiko answered. "Your reputation precedes you."

"*Trio* of Terror?" I looked at Monty. "Maybe we should go on tour?"

Monty gave me a 'don't antagonize the angry lady' look, and shook his head slightly.

"You have been misinformed," Monty said. "There are factions within the Council that would benefit from our removal."

"Are you saying the reports of your destruction are false?"

"No," Monty answered. "But the context of the destruction has been manipulated. The context is decisive."

"Just to be clear," I said, "the TATE deserved and needed remodeling. Have you seen that building? Hideous doesn't begin to describe it."

Monty was spooling energy into his body, which meant things were going to get mage *conversational* in the next few moments. I made sure my mala bead was clear of my sleeve.

"Is that your justification?" Fumiko asked, uncrossing her arms. "The building was ugly?"

"Well, that, and the Consortium started their conversation pretty much the same way you did...only with less manners and more blasting."

I sensed the energy around her increase. Shit, things were slowly spiraling out of control.

"It could be that you and your creature threatened their lives, and they felt they needed to take action," Fumiko answered. "Demons are not pets."

"So much for diplomacy," I muttered under my breath. "You're not really listening."

"You three are a threat to my country, region, and person. If you will not surrender, we are authorized to apprehend you by force. I will ask you one last time. Will you surrender?"

"How about we discuss this over a spot of tea?" I asked. "Isn't that one of the accepted ways to iron out differences here in the land of the rising sun?"

Both Monty and Fumiko turned to stare at me.

The look of utter surprise on his face was priceless. Fumiko, on the other hand, probably felt I was being 'cheeky,' to quote Monty. If she knew how I felt about tea, she would know I was pushing my diplomacy skills to their limit.

Fumiko narrowed her eyes at us, said something in rapid Japanese, bowed, and stepped back.

"Discuss this over a spot of tea?" Monty said, backing up. "She threatens to apprehend us and you suggest tea?"

"You said let's try diplomacy. What did she say?"

"I said diplomacy, not insanity. What makes you think she would sit down for 'a spot of tea'?"

"Just trying to be the adult in the park here," I said. "I didn't call her a creature or insult her. Trust me, the opportunities were there. I showed an enormous amount of restraint."

"*Trio* of Terror was a bit much," Monty said. "It's not like we deliberately go around destroying property. The damage is taken completely out of context."

I stared at him for a second.

"So, that last part…What did she say?"

"She regrets that she will have to eliminate us…or something like that," Monty answered, keeping his eyes on the group in front of us. "Some of it doesn't translate directly, but that is the general gist."

"What are they waiting for?" I asked when I saw Fumiko return to the semicircle of swords. "Are we supposed to attack first? Is that the polite thing to do?"

"Are you suffering effects from the circle?" Monty asked, and started gesturing. "If a battle mage, an allegedly immortal being, and his hellhound appear in your region...what would you do?"

"You mean besides run in the other direction?"

"Pretend that's not an option, and you're part of an organization that is currently in pursuit of said 'Trio of Terror.' What would be your next move?"

"The smart play would call for backup," I said. "Keep them busy until an overwhelming force of help arrived, and then...Shit."

"Yes," Monty said with a nod. "Say one thing, but make sure it has layers of meaning. That is the usual Japanese conversational style."

"She's been stalling this whole time?"

"Three faces—remember the culture."

"One you show everyone, one you show those closest to you, and one you keep hidden," I answered. "Everything is layered here. I forgot how much I enjoyed talking in circles."

"Assessing and determining our level of strength. Her statements were designed to determine our weak points, if any."

"She stepped back because she realized taking us on with her group would be a loss."

"Or at least more of a loss than she was prepared to suffer."

"Are we going to politely allow ourselves to get blasted then?" I asked, as the sun crept over the horizon and illuminated the park fully. "What are we waiting for?"

"I was waiting for that," Monty said, as the sun blazed down upon us. "I needed more light for this."

Monty gestured and clapped his hands together. A white burst of energy shot out from his palms, momentarily blinding me.

"What the hell was that?" I asked, rubbing my eyes. "You're taking magical selfies now?"

"We need to go," Monty said. "Get ready."

"What about—" I started, and stopped when my vision cleared. "What are those?"

All around us, versions of Monty, Peaches and me were moving or entering attack stances. In some of them, Monty was casting runes into the air. In others, Peaches was stalking forward slowly, crawling on his belly in 'predatory pounce' mode. The images were spaced out pretty far from one another.

Fumiko and her group had closed ranks and were keeping their distance.

"Those are simulacra," Monty explained. "They are caused by manipulating light from the visible spectrum into images."

"Can they actually do anything besides freak out Fumiko and her crew?"

"No, it's a distraction to facilitate our exit," Monty answered as he gestured again. A green circle appeared beneath us. Half a second later, green circles appeared beneath all of our copies. "Hard light simulacra take more time and energy. We need to make haste before reinforcements arrive."

"You're stronger than her, aren't you?"

"Yes, but she's no pushover. Her disruption wave targeted your creature," Monty said, glancing at my hellhound. "I just don't know how."

"We could just ask her nicely," I said, glaring at Fumiko. "Maybe use a few orbs of percussive persuasion?"

"Attacking and taking down a regional director of the Dark Council won't make us any friends, here or back home," Monty replied. "Let's subdue the enemy without fighting. I know someone who can look at him and hopefully tell us what she cast."

"The greatest victory is that which requires no battle," I answered with an appraising nod. "Fine. Let's go. Looks like the Dark Council is still upset with you."

"With me?" Monty said. "She did say *Trio* of Terror."

"It should be *Duo* of Devastation," I said, glancing at Peaches. "Can you find us somewhere safe?"

"Relatively, yes," Monty answered. "But it will have to be a short stay."

"Is this going to hurt?"

"Not much, I think."

I prepared for the agony, and gave him a nod.

Monty knelt and touched the teleportation circle. I felt my stomach seize as the park vanished.

NINE

When I could see clearly again, we were standing in the open courtyard of a large home. A gentle breeze caressed my face as I stood still, awaiting the inevitable agony. An almost palpable silence embraced the property, creating a sense of serenity.

It was interrupted every few seconds by the sound of running water and the methodic clunk of a *shishi-odoshi*, a pivoting bamboo tube that filled with water and struck a stone in a steady rhythm. The water feature was situated off to one corner of the property.

The courtyard was enclosed by high walls on all sides. In the corners, I saw several *sakura*—cherry trees in full bloom. In the center of the courtyard was a small pond, to the rear of the pond, off to the side, I saw a zen garden. Most of the courtyard was hidden from view beyond the walls by large black pine trees along the perimeter.

The house itself resembled a smaller version of Osaka castle. Whoever lived here valued their privacy. Along the walls of the courtyard, I could sense the runes; they were a subtle deterrent to approaching the property. On each door, I noticed the large golden circles embedded into the wood. Each door thrummed with a strong energy signature.

"The runes in these walls," I said. "Is it like a polite 'keep out or you get fried' sort of thing?"

"You can sense the runes?" Monty asked, looking at me. "Fascinating."

"Don't go Vulcan on me. What do they mean?"

"You shouldn't be able to sense these runes. They are ancient and embedded into the stone. They are designed to be undetectable."

"Someone did a poor job of hiding them," I said, suddenly grabbing my stomach with a sharp intake of breath. It felt like someone had shoved a hot sword through my midsection and had started dragging it across my abdomen. "How severe is this one going to be?"

Monty looked at me and shook his head as he gestured. Golden runes floated over to where I swayed in pain, landing on me.

"It will be slightly uncomfortable for a short duration."

I took a step and immediately felt my intestines tighten. My knees buckled, and I leaned against one of the cool walls as I slid to the ground. At this point, I half expected some creature to burst out of my body and run skittering away. It was clear Monty and I had differing opinions on what defined discomfort. I looked up and saw Peaches and Monty observing me. Peaches stepped close, his drooling tongue in assault mode. I held out a hand to keep him back.

<Would you like me to lick you?>

<No, boy. I don't want to be in agony and covered in hellhound slobber.>

<It will make you feel better. My saliva is good for you.>

<No, thanks. I'll get past this. Just give me a minute.>

<If you ate more meat, this wouldn't happen to you.>

<Meat isn't the solution to everything, you know.>

<Meat is life. It fixes everything.>

"Why...does this always happen...to me?" I asked with a groan. "And yet, you two seem fine?"

Monty glanced at Peaches, rubbed his chin, and then looked at me.

"Your creature has a singularity of purpose," Monty said. "He is your bondmate, and your protection is his priority...that, and devouring enormous amounts of meat, it seems. He is in complete harmony. Purpose and expression are one."

"And you?" I managed through the blinding pain. "Why...why are you unaffected?"

"I'm a mage. We don't do internal conflicts without dire consequences. As odd as it may seem, my purpose, like your creature's, is singular and clear."

"Are you saying my purpose is unclear?"

"My best theory is that this pain you are suffering is a result of being out of sync with your abilities, which is a direct expression of your purpose."

"What abilities? I'm not a mage and I don't do...I don't do magic."

"You can fire a magic missile, anemic as it is." He glanced down at Ebonsoul. "You choose to wear your weapon in a sheath when you can transport it internally."

"Because it feels wrong," I snapped back. "I'm not going to carry some odd magical weapon inside of me."

"Which you are bonded to."

"Doesn't matter. It stays in the sheath."

"Your lack of acceptance of this new reality is causing chaos within you. Being stubborn doesn't change the facts."

"Facts?" I asked. "Like the fact I'm thousands of miles from home chasing a vampire that probably wants me dead? For what?"

Monty shook his head.

"You are the Chosen of Kali, my shield-bearer—bonded to

Ebonsoul, your creature, and, it would seem—your vampire. You are clearly suffering from a lack of harmony."

"What I'm suffering from is a lack of coffee," I said, reaching for my flask. "A sip of javambrosia will reset all of my harmonic interference."

"No, it won't," Monty said, squinting in the morning sun and looking around. "But, if it makes you feel better, by all means, imbibe."

"Imbibe, I will," I said, getting unsteadily to my feet and pulling out my small, silver flask. The grinning skulls on the surface gave off blue energy as I took a short pull of coffee godliness and felt it give me a warm hug...from the inside. "That —is divine java."

"Literally," Monty answered. "Hel never told you what was in that flask?"

Valhalla Java, aside from being the best coffee I've ever tasted on this planet, enhanced my reflexes, strength, and vitality for a short time. It was NOS for my brain, though I hadn't yet had a chance to test all of its properties.

It was a gift from Hel, the Norse goddess of the underworld. I was certain there were some nasty side effects to drinking too much of it—like degenerative zombification, or sprouting an extra pair of arms.

"Only that I shouldn't drink too much of it all at once."

Actually, the exact words were: don't drink more than a spoonful at once. Since I wasn't clear on which type of spoon was being referenced, I was using soup ladles as my guide. Between my curse and the Valhalla Java, my body recovered rapidly from the teleportation's mangling of my insides. I was feeling better by the second.

"Are you trying to determine how much is too much?" Monty asked, heading to a large door on the other side of the courtyard. "Or is this a 'wait and see' situation? For all you know, you could be drinking some ungodly poison. You do realize it's not coffee, yes?"

"That is a valid point," I said, turning over the flask a few times while examining it.

"What are you doing?"

"You know how in those commercials they always say something like, side effects may include: nausea, intestinal discomfort, headaches, spontaneous disintegration, and fatal brain implosions? Maybe there's some fine print I missed?"

"On the flask itself? Really?"

"Hel—actually Cathain Grobjorn, the brewer of Odinforce, was a little vague with the instructions," I answered, still examining the flask. "Even he wasn't certain what would happen to me over time because of my unique *condition*."

"You didn't think to ask Hel?"

"Have you met Hel? I don't think she's known for her warm conversations. At the time, I think she was in a Ragnarok planning session with Ezra."

"And you think the side-effect warnings are going to be imprinted on the flask somewhere?"

"That's why it's called 'fine print.' Maybe too much Valhalla Java can cause permanent superhuman strength, lightning-quick reflexes, godlike wisdom and other awesomeness?"

"If it does," Monty said, raising an eyebrow, "when do these symptoms begin to take effect?"

"Was that humor?"

"Simply an observation that there has been no demonstrable change in your strength, reflexes, or wisdom. Could be it increases migraines?"

"I don't suffer from migraines or any type of headaches."

"Not you—for those in proximity to you."

"Oh, *that* was humor. You really should warn me next time. The hilarity is unbearable."

"More than likely this Valhalla Java concoction debilitated

your remaining brain cells, prompting you to suggest tea this morning."

"That was me being diplomatic," I answered. "At least Osaka castle is still standing, and we didn't blow up Fumiko and the bankermages. I call that a win-win."

"Speaking of which, we need to make ourselves scarce and figure out how the Kuro Hyogikai knew of our presence."

When we reached the door, he traced a finger around the golden circle in a clockwise direction three times before knocking and waiting.

TEN

A wave of orange energy shimmered across the surface of the door. After a few seconds, a series of runes flared brightly for several seconds before fading out to a dull glow.

A woman just this side of ancient opened the door. She wore a black, flowing gown that reminded me of Quan's robe. It was covered with subtle, violet runes that changed and shifted every few seconds. Her long, black and gray hair was pulled into a bun and the stare behind her glasses was both piercing and soft. It was the look of a warrior—ready and observant.

Monty said something in rapid Japanese, and she bowed. He returned the bow as she stepped to the side, allowing us to enter. He said something else in a dialect I couldn't understand. She glanced momentarily at Peaches, bowed again, and walked silently away into the house.

Even though I could tell she was advanced in age, she had perfect posture and glided effortlessly across the floor. From the way she moved, I knew she was trained—a trained body needed no words to convey its experience. I noticed the small, runed dagger she used to keep her bun in place.

"Who is that?" I looked around the house. "What is this place?"

We stood in a small, foyer-like area. The interior of the space was a mix of modern and antique. The floor was covered with tatami mats, but the light fixtures were state of the art. I saw a touchpad beside the entrance to a room adjacent to the foyer. The place looked old, but the defenses were a mix of runes and modern tech.

"Kiri is the head caretaker of this estate, which is owned by the Golden Circle."

"Isn't this place a little large for her to manage on her own?"

"There are several staff who live on the property. The resident mage is an old friend."

"Is this like a Golden Circle safe-house?"

"Something like that," Monty said, removing his shoes. "This is the Repository. We can't stay long; the defenses are strong, but I have no desire to bring the Kuro Hyogikai or the Blood Hunters to their doorstep. This location is not designed to deal with violence. Jun is a scholar and instructor, not a battle mage."

"I don't know, Kiri looks pretty dangerous to me."

"She is, but her role is to keep Jun and this place safe. Getting them involved in our fight would be the height of impropriety."

"We're worried about being rude?"

"Yes," Monty said. "Jun is a dear friend and mentor. Bringing our enemies to his doorstep is poor form and dangerous to him and the items placed in his care. We will stay for a short while and then vacate the premises."

"Won't the Council assume you would come here first?" I asked, removing my shoes when Monty gave me the mageglare. It registered at least a two on my glare-o-meter, and I quickly stepped out of my footwear before proceeding farther into the space. "It's what I would do."

"They would if they knew where to look," Monty said, heading farther into the house. "This location doesn't remain in one place for long."

"Like the Moving Market?"

"Precisely. The runes you sensed outside allow this entire building to phase in and out of the planes automatically without needing oversight."

"But it's not safe?" I asked. "Doesn't that kind of defeat the whole safe-house idea?"

"The purpose of this location is to serve as a place of training. Golden Circle mages come here to practice some of the more dangerous runes. This isn't a stronghold, and many of the books located here are priceless. Eventually, Esti will find us—the Blood Hunters are determined."

"What happened to the three days Uhura said we would have?"

"Ursula, and that is a good question," Monty said. "Either she wasn't being completely honest, or someone interfered with her circle and our teleport. Both options have the potential to be disastrous."

"Do you think the Kuro what's-its-name would attack here? Wouldn't that piss off the Golden Circle?"

"It's not them I'm concerned about," Monty said. "I need a cuppa."

"I could use some Deathwish, but I'll take whatever passes for coffee here."

"I'm sure you won't be disappointed," Monty said. "Kiri will notify the kitchen staff. Let's go find Mage Manabu. He would be in the training area."

"This mage, Manatee—"

"Manabu. His *name* is Junichi Manabu," Monty answered. "Do not call him a manatee."

"Right, this mage, Malibu, is he like Master Yat?"

"No one is like Master Yat," Monty replied with a shake of his head. "You should know that by now."

"It's just that when you say 'training area' my brain understands the 'inflicting of pain upon my person.'"

"This place is a mage's training area. You will only have pain inflicted upon you if you call him anything other than Manabu."

"Got it," I said. "Mage Manabu it is."

ELEVEN

Monty touched one of the panels next to a plain wall, in one of the rear rooms. The panel slid silently to the side and revealed a narrow, steep set of stairs going down. The majority of Japanese homes didn't have basements, usually because the water table on the island was too high.

Because of that, it was too costly to dig out and seal the space required for a functional basement. Traditional Japanese homes lacked central heating, which meant there was no need for a boiler or furnace. Nonetheless, the stairs I was looking down definitely led to a basement of some kind. Small root cellars were common in Japan—full-blown basements, not so much. We stopped at the top of the stairs. Monty held out a hand, keeping me behind him.

"He's conducting some kind of experiment," Monty said. "Let's give him a moment."

I peeked my head around Monty's hand and peered into the semi-darkness below.

"What kind of experiment requires a basement…in Japan?"

"Knowing Jun, probably the kind that could erase us if we go down there before he's ready."

I backed away from the stairs because the warning in Monty's voice made me pause.

"Is that you Okoru Tatsu?" a voice called from the basement. "Please give me a few minutes."

"What's an okra tots?" I asked with a smirk. "Is that some kind of vegetable code?"

Monty scowled and mumbled something under his breath.

"Sorry?" I asked, knowing it was something he didn't want to share. "I didn't get that."

"*Okoru tatsu* means angry dragon," Monty said with a sigh. "It was a nickname I was given while I studied here."

"Angry dragon?" I asked. "Your nickname was…angry dragon? Let me guess, because of your pleasant disposition? Or your fascinating ability to reconstruct old buildings that were in disrepair?"

"Shut it," Monty said under his breath. "I was much younger and had not learned proper control."

"Seriously? I'm dealing with the controlled Monty now?"

"You have no idea, trust me," Monty said. "I learned most of my advanced rune casting"—he pointed downstairs into the darkness—"down there."

"This basement was made because of you?"

"There were other mages learning here at the same time, you know, not just me."

There was a *thwump* and the walls of the basement bloomed with orange runes. Whatever had just exploded was contained to the lower level beneath the house. Green smoke filled the area at the foot of the stairs, but something prevented the smoke from coming up to our level.

A figure emerged from the smoke and climbed the stairs slowly. Kiri appeared beside us silently, and nearly made me leap down the stairs when she spoke.

"Shall I arrange for the cleaners?" she asked in a quiet voice that filled the room. She turned to look at us. "Breakfast will be served shortly in the dining room."

"The cleaners won't be necessary, thank you," said a short man wearing a robe with the same design as Kiri. "Breakfast sounds absolutely delicious."

Kiri peered down at Junichi, who smiled back.

"Will the building remain intact?" Kiri answered. "Or will we need to reset the foundation—again?"

"Honestly, Kiri," Jun replied, waving her words away. "I was conducting a small temporal experiment. There was no danger, imminent or imagined, to the structure."

"The last 'temporal experiment' had me meeting younger and older versions of you," she said with a huff. "It became tiresome after the first day, not to mention disruptive to my and the Repository's schedule."

"This was nothing like that," Jun answered. "I was merely testing out the annihilation theory of encountering and interacting with a future self. It's coming along quite nicely. I can assure you, no other versions of me will appear."

Kiri nodded and glided away. "We shall see."

"I see she hasn't changed much," Monty said, turning to face Junichi. "You look well, Master Mana—"

"Tatsu!" Junichi interrupted and grabbed Monty by the shoulders. "We've missed you!"

"And I you, Junichi—" Monty started.

"Let me look at you," Junichi interrupted again, squeezing Monty's arms and shoulders. "You're skin and bones. Are you eating?"

I was liking Junichi more by the second. He held Monty out at arm's length and shook his bald head in mock disapproval.

"I'm eating enough," Monty said. "As much as I need."

"He never ate enough," Junichi said, looking at me. "When he did eat, it was salads, legumes, noodles, and maybe miso soup." He turned back to Monty. "I still think you'd be happier if you ate meat every so often." Junichi held up a finger and wagged it at Monty. "There is life in meat."

I tried to suppress a laugh and failed. Peaches had finally found his human counterpart.

"You know very well I can't—" Monty tried again.

"This must be Mr. Strong," Junichi said with a smile, extending a hand palm up. It looked like he was asking for something, but he kept his hand stationary. "Welcome to the Repository."

"Thank you. What do you keep here?" I said, extending my hand into his. "Is this like the Living Library?"

He closed his eyes as he clasped my hand with both of his. A second later, a gentle, golden light formed around our hands like a miniature sun, then disappeared almost as quickly as it had appeared.

"It's similar," Junichi answered. "If Professor Ziller can't find a text, he comes to us. We would most certainly have it. If we don't have it, it doesn't exist."

"You're *the* library to the library?"

"And you are the thrice-bound chosen of Kali," Junichi said, looking down at Peaches. "He is a beautiful specimen."

"This is my hellhound—"

"Peaches," Junichi finished, crouching down and softly rubbing Peaches' head. "The wonderful and destructive hellhound you are bonded to."

<Did you hear that? I'm wonderful.>

<He also said destructive.>

<You say that like it's a bad thing. Will breakfast include meat for the wonderful hellhound?>

"I'm certain you are all hungry," Junichi said, standing. "We have much to discuss, and it's best to discuss these matters over food."

TWELVE

The dining room was a small affair for such a large home. The oak table was low to the ground, with small cushions on each side for seating. Off to one side was a large, metal bowl filled with beef, which I assumed was for the bottomless pit of a hellhound next to me.

<Can I go eat it now? That smells so good.>

<No, wait. We have to have manners. We are guests here.>

<I'm sure the rules are different for a wonderful hellhound. Can I go now?>

"Master Manabu? Can Peaches go—?"

"Please, call me Jun, and of course—please go eat, Peaches. Never a good idea to keep a hungry hellhound waiting."

Peaches padded over slowly, in the greatest show of restraint I had ever seen from him, and proceeded to slowly eat the meat from his bowl. I looked on in awe.

"How did you do that?" I asked.

"Do what?" Jun answered with a smile.

"Get him to actually take his time eating? Usually by now he's inhaled the meat and part of the bowl."

"He used a time—distortion field," Monty said, glancing at Peaches with narrowed eyes. "With a stasis component. It's quite elegant."

Jun gave Monty a short bow. "High praise indeed, Tatsu. Thank you."

"Can you cause one of those time fields when we get home?" I asked, looking at Monty. "That way we can slow down the hellhound-bowl destruction. Titanium isn't cheap, you know."

"Your creature isn't moving any slower in his mind," Monty replied, "but I'm afraid a field of this complexity is beyond me, by at least two or three centuries. Jun is a Temporal Runes master."

"It was worth a try," I said, shaking my head as Peaches slowly ate his food. "Titanium bowls it is."

On the table sat several trays with different kinds of food. On one tray, I saw a small bowl of steamed rice accompanied by another bowl of miso soup. Next to it, in a small dish, was a serving of *natto*, fermented soy beans. Beside it sat a few pieces of grilled salmon, and on the plate next to the salmon, I saw *umeboshi*—pickled plums.

To finish off the presentation, there were a fair amount of vegetable side dishes, some seasoned dried seaweed and a green salad. Most importantly, I noticed the large mug of steaming, black coffee sitting on one corner of the table.

All of this sat on a decorative tray, and each of us had an identical tray in front of us. The food smelled delicious, and I realized just how hungry I had been. Jun grabbed a pair of chopsticks and started eating. Monty followed his example and I reached for the coffee first, taking a slow sip of the luxurious caffeine ink. I let out a soft sigh of pleasure as Monty glanced at me before drinking from a cup of tea with a satisfied sigh of his own.

"I am pleased it meets with your approval," Jun said, placing his chopsticks gently on the *hashi-oki*—the chopstick rests on the side of his tray. "We may be known for tea, but we can appreciate a good cup of coffee when the situation presents itself."

"Jun, we have a situation," Monty said after a few moments. "The hellhound was subjected to a disruption wave."

"I see," Jun said, staring at Peaches. "It's subtle, but effective. Who cast this?"

"Fumiko of the Kuro Hyogikai," Monty answered. "Can you undo it?"

"Not without studying the particular sequence," Jun said, shaking his head. "She has grown in ability."

"What does it do?" I asked. "Will this disruption wave hurt him?"

"It's designed to neutralize your hellhound's abilities," Jun said. "I can cast a counter-rune that should blunt its effects. If you give me a few days, I can undo the original runes."

"A few days?" I asked. "Will he be okay?"

He must have seen the worried expression on my face and patted my shoulder.

"I will need a few days to reverse engineer the runes. The alternative is to get the original caster to undo the casting."

"That's not going to happen," I said. "She didn't seem like the type to take back a casting—at least not without violent persuasion."

"Agreed. The Kuro Hyogikai are single-minded of purpose and stubborn to a fault," Jun answered. "I'm sure she means well."

Jun narrowed his eyes and stared at Peaches for close to ten seconds.

"Can you see the interlacing?" Monty asked. "She's using him as a beacon."

"Yes—it seems she wants to know your location at all times. I can inhibit that aspect of the cast, but the neutralizing component will take a little more to unravel."

"Thank you," I said. "I don't want anything happening to him."

"Hellhounds are very resilient creatures," Jun answered with a smile. "Very little affects them. This casting was creative in that it used his own defenses against him. They must have been expecting you. It's a very specific cast."

"Does this mean he's vulnerable to these kinds of castings?" I asked. "I thought he'd be immune to this sort of thing?"

"He is still young," Jun said. "His defenses are still developing. Whoever taught Fumiko this sequence is quite accomplished in dealing with otherworldly beings. This type of casting will not work when he gets a little older."

"This can be a serious problem," Monty said. "If she tries to track us—"

"You have several problems," Jun answered calmly. "Let's start with the immediate and move outward from there."

Monty nodded. "Simon's vampire left the Dark Council and—"

"No," Jun said. "That is not immediate, Tatsu." He looked at me. "Simon—if I may call you Simon—what do you perceive as the immediate problem?"

I gave it some thought. Chi had left the Dark Council, and that was a choice with long-term consequences. It was true that the Council could tear itself apart, but that wasn't going to happen overnight.

Ken, Erik, the NYTF, and other players in the city would prevent that implosion—at least initially. The Dark Council was a check and balance against greater devastation, as imperfect as it was.

The threat had to be closer—and then I saw it.

"The blades," I said. "The bond to the blades is the immediate problem."

"Why?" Jun asked. "Why should the blades be your immediate concern?"

"Esti and the Blood Hunters are coming for those first," I said. "It will reestablish their power base and make every other faction take notice."

"They can't just *take* the blades, though," Monty said. "Both you and Grey are bonded to the weapons. To break the bond means to kill you first."

"Out of the two, I'm the harder target," I said. "Why come after me?"

"You have a vulnerability the Warden does not," Jun answered. "Do you know what it is?"

"Chi," I said. "My connection to her makes me vulnerable."

"Does it?" Jun asked. "Is that your real vulnerability?"

Jun looked to the side and focused on the politely chomping Peaches.

"Yes," I said. "My bond to Ebonsoul also happens to be a bond to Chi."

Jun nodded. "If they target her and she flees—" he began.

"They knew I would come after her," I finished.

"Why?" Jun asked. "She is a vampire, and you are not."

"She's the leader of the Dark Council."

"Which has vowed to eliminate you and your hellhound, and hurt your friend."

"I need to know," I said after a pause. "She's not evil. I know her. There has to be another reason for her behavior."

"Do you believe this to be the case, Tatsu?" Jun turned to face Monty. "You think this vampire has good in her?"

"I believe she cares for Simon and has demonstrated that more than once."

"But you are not certain."

"I'm certain that if she poses a threat to those under my protection, I will eliminate her."

Jun nodded. "Elements within the fractured Dark Council have maneuvered you all here. Do you know why?"

"They make her leave the city—we follow, and they isolate us from any kind of external protection or assistance."

"In Go, it is called a cut," Jun said. "They have succeeded in removing you from any support in order to eliminate you."

"What could they say to make her leave the Dark Council?"

"You will have to ask her when you find her."

"If Hades hadn't been so generous, we could have bargained with at least one of the blades," Monty said. "As it stands, we will need to stop them on three fronts now, instead of two."

"Hades is playing a much longer game than we can see," Jun replied. "By giving the Night Warden the blade, he has created flux in what was once a static situation."

"Ugh, gods and their games," I said. "All he had to do is keep the sword safe and give it back—to Monty. Why was that so hard?"

"He wanted to create a state of chaos," Monty said. "What I don't know is why."

"What he created is a nightmare," I said. "For that matter, why would Chi give me a blade that was designed to kill and siphon supernaturals?"

"Because she knew the day would come when it would be needed," Jun said. "She wanted to make sure that whoever held that blade would not be swayed by power or status."

"All she did was make my life harder," I said. "Now I have to deal with Esti and her psychogroup of hunters."

"You could always let them kill you," Jun answered. "That would sever the bond, at least in theory."

"I did the whole dying thing in London. Thanks, but no thanks. I came back and the bond was still there. I think, in order to sever this particular bond, it needs to be a final death —which isn't an option when one of my bonds is to a hellhound."

"Indeed. Severing that bond would result in catastrophe."

"That's a nice way of saying an unstoppable XL Hellhound would destroy the city," I said. "True death is the only way I can see my bond with Ebonsoul breaking."

"Hmm," Jun said, tapping his chin. "That would make sense. Your bonds, especially the ones associated with the blade, are inextricably linked to the vampire. It's very possible you *both* must die to sever that bond."

"Wonderful, I'll make sure to let Esti know she has to kill me *and* Chi."

"I think that's the plan in either case," Monty answered. "You recall the situation your vampire was in when you killed Anastasia?"

"I do. They were planning to give Chi the ultimate suntan. She should've never given me this blade."

"I'd say she chose well," Jun said. "She gave the blade to an immortal with a conscience who, at least until now, has not gone on a rampage in the quest for more power."

"If the blades are the immediate concern, that makes the Dark Council a close second," Monty said. "They want to eliminate Simon and his creature as well as erase my abilities."

"Do they?" Jun asked with a slight smile. "Then why haven't they done so?"

"What do you mean?" I asked. "They are after us."

Jun stood slowly, but gracefully, unfolding his legs. I got to my feet with about as much grace as a newborn foal. Pins and needles shot down both my legs as my lower body woke up from sitting in *seiza:* an upright kneeling position, one which compressed the nerves in my legs.

"The Dark Council is a global organization," Jun said as he led us out of the dining room and down a long hallway. "Do you really think there is anywhere on this planet you could go where they wouldn't be able to eventually find you?"

"No," Monty said, pensively. "The DCE has counterparts everywhere. If they wanted, they could hunt us down. Not easily, but given their resources, it would only be a matter of time."

"Then it stands to reason that someone in the Dark Council is aiding your progress and wants you to do what they cannot."

"Get killed so that Esti and her group can get Ebonsoul?" I asked. "Because that is not on my to-do list...ever."

"They want you to remove the threat of the Blood Hunters," Jun said. "It also seems that someone would prefer you die in the process. Do not pretend everyone in the Council wants you to succeed. You have many adversaries."

"Well, that makes me feel all kinds of cozy and loved," I said. "Do you know who else we can contact in the Dark Kuro-thing here?"

"The Kuro Hyogikai is led by Fumiko in this area. She is the regional director and an accomplished mage."

"She is much stronger than she appears," Monty said. "She was masking her energy signature effectively."

Jun nodded. "Do not underestimate her. If you outwitted her this time, she will learn from your interaction and prepare a better snare for you next time."

"She is quite the tactician—she almost trapped us," Monty answered. "She revealed her hand with the disruption wave."

"Great," I said. "We can't use deadly force on the Dark Kuro guys, *and* we have to avoid them while dealing with Blood Hunters, who want us dead."

Jun looked up suddenly and then closed his eyes. "Your pursuers are close. We are near our next phasing. Tatsu, would you like me to assist? It has been decades since my last mage battle."

"No," Monty said. "We will use the courtyard exit. Thank you for the meal, Junichi. As always, you have lent me your clarity of thought."

"And as always, it has been my honor," Jun said, and then looked at me. "You have much to discover. The first is to embrace your purpose—once you do that, you will alleviate much of your pain and suffering."

"And the second?"

"You still don't understand why you are more vulnerable than the Warden," Jun said. "When you do, you will discover your greatest strength. I only hope you do so in time."

I nodded. "Thank you," I said, not understanding a word he's said. "I'll make sure to do that."

"No, you won't, not for some time," Jun answered with a chuckle. "But, eventually you will. And when you do, your power will flow unblocked."

THIRTEEN

Jun escorted us outside to the serene courtyard and hugged Monty.

"Please be careful, Tatsu," he said. "This Blood Hunter, Esti… There are rumors. You cannot reason or negotiate with her. She is blinded by revenge and by a quest for power."

"We don't intend to negotiate," Monty said. "We intend to neutralize the threat—permanently."

Jun nodded and reached into his robe. He handed each of us a small golden ring, around three inches wide. The rings were covered in delicate runework that shimmered in the light. It was surprisingly heavy for such a small item. I felt the energy pulse through it as it rested in my palm.

"If you ever find yourself in a situation where you need to get to safety and can't cast, these will bring you here if we are in phase. Make sure they are not activated in proximity to each other. Overlapping portals can cause…rifts."

"Rifts?" I asked, looking at the ring he gave me. "What kind of rifts?"

"Temporal rifts—nasty things that disrupt spacetime. Just be careful activating them. You need at least five feet between the portals."

I looked at the ring with a newfound sense of apprehension.

Monty tried to return his ring to Jun. "We can't accept these. How many portal rings are left?"

"We still have a few left, here and elsewhere," Jun answered, pushing Monty's hand back. "I can't take them back. They have been keyed to your signatures"—he looked at me—"and even to your Peaches. Which reminds me…"

Jun knelt down next to Peaches and placed his hands on the hellhound's sides. He muttered something under his breath, and a red-violet glow surrounded Peaches.

"You encased him in a multi-phasic shell?" Monty said with a hint of awe. "Your temporal skills have increased. I recall you positing this theory. Has my uncle seen this?"

"Not yet," Jun said with a smile. "He will, when we swing by the Golden Circle later this month."

"How long will it remain stable?" Monty asked, stepping close to Peaches. "This is beyond anything I've ever seen."

"It will be stable for a few days, and then it will degrade slowly. That should prevent any effects of the disruption wave."

"Thank you, Jun," I said with a bow. "I don't know how to repay you."

"Stay safe, keep Tatsu safe, and protect your Peaches," Jun said, rubbing Peaches behind the ears, before standing and walking back to the door. "That will be payment enough."

<Did you thank him for your meat?>

<Should I lick him?>

<How about a nudge? One that doesn't send him flying, and doesn't break anything.>

Peaches padded over and bumped his head into Jun's leg, nearly knocking him down. He finished off with a low bark that almost shattered my eardrums.

Jun laughed. "You're welcome," he said, rubbing Peaches behind the ears again. "Please visit if you can."

<How was that?>

<We need to work on your thank-yous. My ears can barely take it when you speak.>

<If you ate more, it wouldn't bother you.>

<I don't think meat can help protect my ears from you.>

<Frank says it's important to leave a depression when you meet people.>

<I think he meant an impression.>

<The happy man is laughing. I think he liked my thank-you. It means I made a good depression.>

"I'm sorry about that," I apologized. "He doesn't know his own strength sometimes. Thank you again for the portal ring, and...everything."

Jun waved my words away and turned his head as if hearing something behind him.

"The phase is starting, and the hunters are on their way," Jun said. "I'm sorry we can't be of more assistance."

"You've given us more assistance than you can imagine," Monty answered. "Please get the Repository safe now. We will deal with this threat."

Jun hugged Monty again and closed the door behind us. Seconds later, we were alone as the building disappeared, making the courtyard an open U-shaped space.

"We could have just stayed with him and phased away," I said, looking at the empty space that had been occupied seconds earlier. "That would've provided us more assistance."

"No," Monty answered, gesturing. "Our signatures reduce their ability to remain hidden. Aside from the fact that he isn't a battle mage, he must keep his location hidden—that is his primary responsibility. Some of the books in the Repository are priceless and the only remaining copies in existence."

"Well, then," I said, drawing Grim Whisper and shaking out my wrist to give myself access to my mala bracelet. "Let's get ready to have a conversation with some psychohunters."

FOURTEEN

The energy around the courtyard shifted. Peaches let out a deep rumble and shifted into 'tear and shred' mode. The runes in the walls around us were dormant.

"What happened to the runes?" I asked as Monty kept gesturing. "I don't sense them anymore."

"We have hunters incoming," Monty said, glancing down at Peaches. "If Esti is leading them, you will need to destabilize her."

"She's already destabilized," I said. "You want her off the deep end. She's still deadly."

"Irrational and deadly is easier to face than rational and deadly."

"Does that really exist—rational and deadly? We have yet to meet someone who wants to blast us to little bits while presenting a rational reason why."

"No one comes to mind at the moment," Monty said, gesturing one last time. "We really need to expand our circle of adversaries."

"How about we shrink it instead? To zero?" I asked with a shake of my head. "Back to the runes in the wall—did you break them?"

The white runes he traced in the air floated away from us in every direction, landing in different parts of the courtyard and fading from sight. I noticed the pond and zen garden had disappeared as well. Only the large black pine trees remained, encircling the perimeter of the courtyard like silent sentinels.

"The runes and decorative features of the courtyard are only active and present when the Repository is in place," Monty said. "They are currently giving off a subtle but powerful 'nothing to see here and stay away' suggestion to normals. Otherwise, it would attract too much attention."

I nodded. It made sense. The runes would keep the property clear of curious onlookers. The Blood Hunters would arrive and barely raise an eyebrow from people in the surrounding area—the runes in the courtyard acted like blinders to whatever happened on the property.

"How do you want to do this? Diplomacy?"

"This isn't the Kuro Hyogikai," Monty said, reaching behind him and drawing one of the Sorrows. "The Blood Hunters, and Esti especially, want you dead. Today, diplomacy will be at the edge of a sword."

"You don't absorb your swords, do you?" I asked. "I mean, you reach back, and poof—there they are, but I don't see them turning into mist or anything."

"I keep them in a trans-dimensional sheath," Monty said. "They are not like your blade or the sword Grey now wields. Think of them as being in a large pocket only I can access."

"Can you create a pocket like that for Ebonsoul?"

"I'm afraid not," Monty said, shaking his head. "The composition of your blade would prevent it. In addition, I'm not bound to the Sorrows. These are mere weapons—not siphons."

"Don't know about the 'mere weapon' part," I said. "I've seen those things in action."

"They are formidable, but they are only as effective as the wielder," he said, holding up one of the blades as it released a small cry. "In the end, they are still only weapons, dependent on my skill. Your blade is—more."

"Are you sure you can still use those things?" I asked, looking at him warily. "I know you had them recently upgraded to seraphs, but you haven't been fighting with them, and Blood Hunters aren't demons."

Monty rolled his shoulders and swung the sword in front of him. Each practice cut he executed sounded like the weeping of a young girl. Not creepy at all.

"It hasn't been that long since London," he said with a few more practice cuts. "I'm sure it'll come back to me."

Monty reached back and removed the second blade, holding it out, checking the balance. Black runes covered the silver blades on both sides. The hilt was the figure of a young woman with her arms outstretched to the sides.

When Monty extended the sword, the figure's arms wrapped loosely around his wrist, forming a guard and protecting him. He rested his arms at his side as the twin blades gave off a soft wail.

"Have I told you how creepy those things are?"

"Yes, you have," Monty answered. "Are they any less creepy than a blade that can potentially kill a god?"

"Point taken," I said, adjusting Ebonsoul in its sheath. "I'm guessing we're not unleashing orbs of destruction today?"

Monty shook his head. "The courtyard is covered with runic triggers," he said. "Any active magic used will be met with a swift response. The runes won't distinguish who is doing the casting. Think of them as runic proximity mines."

"Runic triggers? Blood Hunters don't use active magic."

"They won't use LIT rounds on us; that would be a waste of ammunition."

"Since we aren't vampires. Makes sense—Light Irradiated Tungsten would hurt, but it would be a waste. LIT rounds aren't cheap."

"They can, however, use erasure rounds, and your favorite—"

"Blood arrows," I said. The last time I dealt with one up close, it was buried in my leg. "Not a fan of blood arrows or erasure rounds."

"Nor am I," Monty agreed. "Both of those will trigger the runes I released around us. I'd suggest no magic missiles, Or overt rune use." He looked down at my bracelet. "Your shield should be fine, though."

I looked down at the mark on my hand. "I'm guessing activating my mark would be a bad idea?"

"What part of 'runes all around us' is unclear?"

"What about null swords?" I asked, making sure Ebonsoul was handy. I realized this was a nervous tic, but there was no way I was going to absorb the thing. "Last time I faced a Blood Hunter —Anastasia—she had a null sword that was not fun."

"That's what my Sorrows are for," Monty answered. "They also have a passive sonic defense, hence the wails."

"Won't her sword set off the triggers? I mean its active energy."

"It's active non-energy. A null sword will read like a void. Would you like me to explain the interaction of energies between the triggers and a null artifact?"

"Not really, no. I get the gist of it. Null sword won't activate the triggers. Watch out for blood arrows and don't get cut or shot."

"Make sure your creature avoids them as well," Monty said. "I don't know what could happen if he's hit by either, considering his defenses are currently compromised."

"Basically: Take them down, don't get hit, stabbed, or shot."

"That about sums it up," Monty said with a short nod. "Avoid the null blade, especially. Do not let it cut you."

"Wasn't planning on it," I said, checking Grim Whisper.

"Use your gun or your blade—no runic energy. The runic triggers are for the Blood Hunter runes in addition to their weapons. Once they activate their runes—"

"Boom?"

"No. The triggers are percussive, not explosive," Monty said. "We only need to stop Esti to derail the hunters."

"I hope you're right," I said. "They certainly aren't going to be worrying about our well-being."

Monty looked at Grim Whisper. "Your ammunition?"

"I'm using persuaders, because a group of dead Blood Hunters in a courtyard sounds like a recipe for meeting whatever passes for the NYTF in Japan. Even with 'stay away' runes, dead bodies tend to attract attention."

"Converting the courtyard into a cemetery will certainly alert the authorities. Best to avoid that scenario."

"Will I explode if I use persuaders?"

"It should be fine," Monty said after a moment of thought. "They act on a delay, which means any runic activity is released *after* they hit their target. Erasure rounds and blood arrows are active and radiate a constant runic energy signature."

"Have you tested this theory?"

"No, but the theory is sound," Monty said. "I even compensated for your creature using his abilities."

"Meaning?"

"He shouldn't set off the runic charges if he phase shifts while he attacks."

"Shouldn't—meaning there's a chance it can happen?"

"Every time runes are used there is a degree of risk. Energy manipulation is dangerous and volatile. You should know this by now."

"I do. I'm just noticing that we do the volatile and dangerous thing more often than not," I said. "Now I know why the Repository needed a basement. What about your Sorrows? Aren't they active?"

"Not unless I want them to be, but nothing in life is guaranteed."

"Except pain," I said. "My life has guaranteed pain."

"Well, that's because you're special," Monty said with an almost smile. "Energy is not always an exact science, despite the fact that mages think they can control it. Many times, they cannot."

"You don't know how scary that sentence sounds," I said seriously.

"Actually, I do."

"You're saying there's a chance my gun can explode, your swords might detonate, and my hellhound can end up in small bits if he phases—is that about right?"

"We will be fine," Monty said. "Have you ever seen anything that can hurt a hellhound? Jun protected him, you're immortal, and I have control over my blades."

"He is indestructible as far as I can tell," I said, looking down at the growling Peaches. "Although London wasn't fun."

"Fun is not the word I would use, no."

I flashed back to the time Thomas Rafael, a mage and frenemy of Monty's, tried to kill Peaches by poisoning him. Almost losing him wasn't a pleasant memory.

<Bad people are coming>

<I know, boy. These bad people will try to hurt you.>

<Can I bite them?>

<Yes, shake, but no chewing. They will be protected. Just don't get hit.>

<I will go in-between.>

<Good plan. Monty and I will stop them.>

Several large, black trucks raced down the street and stopped at the newly formed entrance of the courtyard. I noticed, then, that we were in a dead-end and they had just blocked the only exit. By placing the runic triggers and standing at the end farthest from the opening, we were enticing the Blood Hunters to come to us.

We were using ourselves as bait by standing in what

amounted to a box-canyon kill box. This was going to be an exercise in percussive pain.

"Maybe we can convince her to stop this insanity," I said, realizing how crazy my words sounded as they escaped my lips. "Maybe she'll listen to reason."

"Always a possibility," Monty said with a nod. "I'm sure Esti just wants to have a small chat. That's why she brought so many Blood Hunters with her."

I looked and saw two more trucks pull up before more Blood Hunters poured out of them. This was going to get bloody, fast.

"Fine," I said. "Let's go help her see the error of her ways."

We walked forward to meet Esti and her Blood Hunters.

FIFTEEN

"Surrender," Esti said from across the courtyard.

Around her I counted no less than twenty Blood Hunters, all holding some kind of weapon. The six holding swords flanked Esti and walked forward with her. Another six fanned out near the entrance of the courtyard to either side and drew bows. I saw the remaining eight spread out near the trucks and take positions with rifles.

"Time to unleash your unique charm," Monty muttered next to me. "The more crazed she is, the better our chances."

"I'm on it."

<Stay back until I tell you, boy. Don't let them touch you.>

<They smell bad.>

<When I say, you get the ones in the back with the long guns first.>

<I'm ready. Can we get meat after this? The wag-you kind?>

<We're in the perfect place for it. Yes, I'll get you extra Wagyu meat afterward.>

Esti was dressed very much like the last time I saw her. She wore what appeared to be a black bodysuit—it was overlaid with sections of ballistic armor that covered parts of her body. Over the left side of her suit, I saw a blood—red emblem designating her rank. I figured it meant 'head psycho hunter.'

Her face, neck, and arms, like all of the Blood Hunters, appeared to be covered with some kind of camouflage paint, but it was really a group of photosensitive runic designs.

From a distance, it looked like they had been dipped in black ink. Her black hair was cut short on one side and long on the other, covering one side of her face. Beneath the hair covering her face I could see wisps of black energy wafting around her.

"You've decided to surrender?" I asked. "Who said you weren't smart? We accept."

"I'm going to enjoy watching you die, Strong," Esti said, drawing her black blade and walking toward us. "Right after I gut your vampire and bake her carcass in the sun. Would you like me to save some of the ash? I can spread it over your corpse, and you can finally be together."

"Seems like we got off on the wrong foot," I said, taking a step back. "I'd love to give you the blade, but that's going to be a little complicated. Have you been working out?"

She glared at me. Easily a one on the glare-o-meter, but off the charts on the psycho scale. The lights were on, but no one was even near the house—they weren't even in the same neighborhood.

"For the death of Anastasia Anyxia Santiago, former leader of the *Cazadoras Sangrientas*—the Blood Hunters—I pass judgment and find you guilty."

Esti was unstable on a good day. Today, I needed her irrational.

"Guilty of what?" I asked. "Anastasia tried to kill me, you know."

"Guilty of *what*?" Esti spat. "Vampires are a sickness—a disease. One that needs to be eliminated from the face of the earth. Anastasia was fulfilling her duty of cleansing your city, and you killed her."

"She and I just disagreed on the whole 'removal of essential body parts' argument. I'd say I managed to come out ahead in that conversation—unlike Nick."

"You deserve to die, just like he did. You deserve to have your arms and legs sliced off, your tongue ripped from your throat, and a dagger plunged into your heart repeatedly."

"That's pretty medieval of you," I said. "I'm flattered."

"I'm going to kill everything and everyone you care about," she said with a smile. "Then I'm going to kill you, you vampire-lover."

"Tell me how you really feel," I said, drawing Grim Whisper without making any sudden movements. I *was* conscious of how many weapons were pointed my way. "This doesn't have to go down this way."

"There is no other way, Strong. How could you side with them? They feed on humans. You would turn on humanity to protect them? They're monsters."

"You know, in my short time exploring this fringe world of the supernatural and the mostly unbelievable—runes, energy manipulation, mages, vampires, werewolves, gods, and more—I've learned that some of the worst monsters, the most dangerous ones"—I glared at her—"look very human."

"You would protect them and forsake humanity?"

"No, I would protect them against your madness that would hunt them because of what they are," I replied, making sure my mala bracelet was free, "the same way I stop them from hunting humans. You do know not all of them feed on humans."

"Oh, you're standing up for the good vampires? Do you hear yourself? There are no good vampires, unless they're burning and turning to ash!"

There was no reasoning with her, but I had known this from the beginning. Her ideal reality was a vampire-free world, and nothing I said would convince her otherwise.

She was too far gone down her path of vampire cleansing, but

I knew one thing about Esti—she wouldn't stop after the vampires. There would be other threats that needed removing after them. Her kind of crazy never specialized.

"Killing me and Michiko will achieve what? There are others who will stop you."

She laughed as I looked into her eyes and stared into the abyss of madness. Esti had left mildly insane long ago and had entered full-blown psychotic sociopathy—also known as batshit crazy.

"Killing you will get us one step closer. We'll take care of the dark mage later and retrieve the second blade. Killing that bitch, Michiko? That's just plain enjoyment. She deserves death a thousand times over, and I'm going to make sure she suffers before the end."

"When did you become judge, jury, and executioner?"

"The moment that scum, and every other monster like her, decided humans were food," Esti answered, the madness in her eyes screamed oblivion. "Have you made your peace, Strong?"

"You can fool yourself and the rest of these confused Hunters"—I pointed to the stabby-looking hunters that flanked her—"who follow you, but your kind of crazy is familiar."

"Don't call me crazy," Esti said with a hiss. "I'm not crazy."

"Cruel, petty narcissists with delusions of grandeur, like you, are never in short supply," I answered. "What surprises me is how far you *crazy* fucks get before someone puts you in the ground—where you belong."

"Don't. Call. Me. Crazy."

"What about Monty?" I asked, changing gears. "Will you let him go? What about my hellhound?"

Esti looked at Monty as if seeing him for the first time. She glanced from him to Peaches and smiled. It was the smile that sealed the deal for me—she had stepped so far over the edge there was no turning back. In that moment, I had clarity of thought.

Esti needed to die.

"I won't let them go, Strong," she said as black flames engulfed her sword. "But I promise to give them peace."

"No, thanks," Monty said, moving forward and raising his swords. "I have enough peace to last me several lifetimes."

<Now, boy!>

I pressed my mala bead, materializing my shield, raised Grim Whisper, took aim, and all hell broke loose.

SIXTEEN

The Blood Hunters holding the bows did what came naturally, and activated the runes on their bodies.

That was a mistake.

They were slammed into the walls of the courtyard as their runes activated the runic triggers Monty had placed in the area. I heard the impressive thuds as they collided with the brick walls at high speed. Peaches winked out of sight and reappeared near the trucks with an ear-shattering bark.

Esti moved fast, leaving the other sword hunters behind as she closed the distance between us with a slash. Monty slid in front of us and parried her attack. I rolled to the side and drew Ebonsoul as an arrow whistled past my head. I kept my shield up and fired at the rifle hunters in the back. Peaches kept blinking in and out crunching on weapons and disappearing before the Hunters could get their bearings on him.

The sword hunters stayed back, forming a line of blades between us and the hunters near the entrance to the courtyard. Esti was going to face us alone.

Monty lunged with a thrust, moving his gleaming blade in a blazing attack. Esti twisted to the side, deflected one of the

Sorrows, and unleashed a kick that Monty barely managed to block in time. The force of the blow sent him flying back several feet with a grunt.

"You *have* been working out," I said, turning to fire at her.

She whirled on me and unleashed a crescent kick, removing Grim Whisper from my hand, nearly shattering my wrist in the process. I brought up Ebonsoul just in time to stop another horizontal slash. The black flames of the null sword were a little too close for comfort.

"I am a Blood Hunter, Strong," she said through gritted teeth as I grabbed her arm. It felt like squeezing a steel cable. "I'm faster, stronger, and more powerful than you will ever be."

"Funny," I said with a grunt as I tried to keep her from breaking free, realizing she was right on the *stronger* part, "Anastasia said something like that right before I sliced her throat and ended her."

I saw the rage flit behind her eyes as she hissed at me.

"You are a stupid man," she said, unleashing a spear hand at my throat that would have destroyed my larynx.

I dodged and stepped back. "I prefer to see myself as intelligence-challenged," I said, looking for an opening and staying away from her lethal sword.

I shifted to the side as she compensated, aiming a palm-heel strike designed to shatter my chest. I'd have had a set of broken ribs had I not raised the shield at the last second. The strike shoved me back and nearly broke my forearm. It was like being on the receiving end of a wrecking ball, an angry, crazed, Blood Hunter wrecking ball.

"Ouch," I said with a grunt, rubbing my arm as my body flushed hot. "If this Blood Hunter thing doesn't work out, you could always do MMA. We could call you Esti the Testy."

"The lattice!" she yelled, ignoring me. "I'm going to kill you, Strong, but you're going to suffer first."

In the rear I saw another group of Blood Hunters spill out of a truck, holding what looked like a large net.

"You going fishing?" I asked warily as Monty raced back at Esti. "What's the net for? You think you can stop us with a net? You're crazier than I thought."

"Who said anything about *stopping* you?" Esti said, unleashing a barrage of kicks and slashes that kept Monty and me back. "We need you *dead* not stopped you idiot."

"That…almost hurt my feelings," I said, closing the distance. "You do realize a net can't hurt me."

"In the larger scheme of things, you are both insignificant," Esti said, dodging a thrust by Monty. She rotated around the attack and ended up behind him, slicing down with the null sword to cut him in half. Without turning, Monty raised the Sorrows in time to stop the downward attack. "By the time you realize what is happening, it will be too late. We know you, Strong. Better than you know yourself."

"You don't know me," I said, closing with Ebonsoul. "But let me introduce you to my blade."

Esti laughed and maneuvered Monty between us. "You're always out of your league and out of your depth. You are a liability."

"Simon," Monty said, struggling to hold both swords in a cross block as Esti slashed down. "Your…creature."

"My what?" I said, for a moment not making the connection. "What are you talking about?"

"Mage," Esti said with a grimace as she kept bringing her sword down. "Did you think we wouldn't sense your amateurish traps? We've been hunting vampires for centuries. Creatures that are ten times faster, stronger, and more cunning than you will ever be. Your runic triggers are meaningless. We were expecting them."

Another group of Blood Hunters poured out of another truck.

These weren't part of the initial group, and they all carried what looked like machine guns. Behind them I saw a smaller group cast blue orbs into the courtyard. The orbs rolled into the entrance of the courtyard, merged together, and formed a large, shimmering blue sphere of energy that then began to shrink slowly.

"Shit, you guys have mages? Totally not fair. I mean, at least give us a warning."

"Sorceresses," Esti spat. "Not weak, ineffective mages."

Esti backflipped away from us and held the null sword in front of her like a shield. The hunters holding the machine guns opened fire, none of their rounds hitting Esti as she raced back to the trucks. Almost as one, the rest of the hunters started moving back to the trucks.

Monty kept the swords in a cross block and uttered words under his breath. Bullets raced at him and fell to the side as the wails increased. I raised my mala shield just in time to stop the hunter bullets from punching holes into me as they switched targets between Monty and me. In the distance I could see Peaches still mangling hunters and shredding their guns.

"What the hell?" I muttered under my breath as the bullets kept us back. "They're retreating?"

<Come back, boy! It's too dangerous!>

"Simon, call him back, now!" Monty said as the wails increased. "He's in danger."

"I'm trying!" I yelled over the wails of the swords. "He's not responding. I don't think he can hear me through the dome."

Esti laughed as she ran away. "Now, take it!"

Inside the blue sphere, the last group of hunters grabbed the net and tossed it at Peaches, who was busy destroying one of the rifles and slamming a hunter into the wall. The lattice landed on him and immediately exploded in a burst of violet light. Peaches went down with a whine.

"Peaches!" I yelled and moved to close the distance. I pressed the mark on my hand and realized my error. White light shot out from the top of my left hand, as Monty's words crashed into my brain—one nanosecond too late.

Runes all around us.

"Simon, no!" Monty yelled running to my side. "The triggers!"

"Oh, shi—" I managed before the triggers around me went off and launched me back—away from the hunters and away from Peaches. I saw Monty slam into one of the side walls and fall to the ground, unconscious. The Sorrows disappeared a second later.

I crashed into the back wall—hard. Hard enough to shatter the brick with my body. I felt bones break, followed by searing pain. Warmth flushed my body as the pain squeezed the air from my lungs a second later.

Through the haze of my rapidly tunneling vision, I saw Peaches being loaded into one of the trucks by the hunters as Esti approached me.

"You may be immortal, but your hellhound isn't," Esti said as she crouched down by my head. "If you want him back in one piece, bring me the vampire."

I tried to form the words, but the message from my brain to my mouth was getting detoured. I groaned in response.

"I realize you don't know where we will be"—she reached behind her—"but as I understand it, you share a bond with that creature. Once you have the vampire, bring her to us. You have five days. Then I unleash your creature on this city."

She brought her arm down and buried a blood arrow into my right shoulder.

"Fuck...fuck you," I managed and spit up blood. "You are making a mistake."

"Eloquent as usual," Esti said with a laugh as she walked away. "I wouldn't waste time. I hear hellhounds get positively monstrous when they aren't fed and tortured."

"I'm going...I'm going to kill you...slow."

"Promises, promises."

"Give him back," I said. "You don't know...you don't know what you're doing."

She stopped and turned. "I *do* know what I'm doing, Strong. It's called revenge, and reclaiming what's ours. Judging from the way you came at us today, I'm guessing you thought you were the harder target. You were wrong. We've been studying you—your defenses are laughable."

"Studying me?"

"You're vulnerable in ten different ways," she said, looking back to the van where they loaded Peaches as it pulled away. "This was just one of the easier methods to exploit your weaknesses."

"You're going to regret doing this," I said. "It's not too late to give him back and stop this."

"Are you threatening me?" she asked, stepping close to where I lay redecorating the courtyard with my blood. She crouched down, smiled and pushed down on the arrow in my shoulder. I groaned in pain while she laughed slowly. "You're in no position to threaten me."

"It's not a threat," I said, clenching my jaw against the agony. "I will find you and dust your psycho, crazy ass."

Her expression became dark, and she pressed down harder, twisting the arrow as I screamed.

"This is just the start of your suffering, Strong. I'm going to make sure you see your vampire bitch die first, before I kill everyone and everything in your life."

"You have a real hard-on for Chi," I said with a gasp when I could see straight again. "I thought you went after all vampires. Why her?"

"Ask her when you find her."

"I'm not a vampire. This isn't my fight."

"You possess one of our blades, killed one of ours, and allied yourself with our sworn enemy. Did you think we were going to *forget?* Did you think we would forgive your actions…your arrogance?"

"Chi gave me this blade."

"It wasn't *hers* to give," she replied, standing, the anger clear in her voice. "Those blades belong to the Blood Hunters. They are ours—and we *will* get them back."

"Let Peaches go," I said. "You have no idea what he's capable of doing."

"Be careful with the blood arrow," she said, turning and walking away again. "I'd hate to hear you went to pieces over this."

"You're dead. You just don't know it yet."

"Bring me the vampire so we can end this, Strong. I promise it will be agonizing."

"Give him back."

"Do as you're instructed, and it will all be over soon," she said. "Like you said: this isn't your fight."

"You made it my fight the moment you took Peaches. I won't be showing you the same mercy I showed Anastasia."

She stopped walking for a moment.

"I'll be waiting."

Only one truck remained. I saw her get in and watched it vanish down the street.

SEVENTEEN

I noticed the scent first: lotus blossoms. It was a particularly citrus-heavy smell, like a freshly squeezed orange or lemon. This was mixed with a hint of cinnamon and reminded me of my youth—stealing cinnamon sticks from the kitchen to chew on, with a sweet and biting sensation that filled my mouth with each stick.

All of this was enveloped by the smell of freshly turned earth after a hard rain: musty, humid, and reminiscent of cut grass. Around me, the day shifted slowly out of focus as time slid to a halt. That, or I had one hell of a concussion.

"Oh, hell," I said, groaning with the anticipation of more pain. "This day just keeps getting better."

A pair of heels entered my field of vision. I noticed the red soles and figured that whoever was paying me a visit at least had decent taste in shoes. I wasn't going to assume it was Karma, not with the day I was having.

"Splinter," I heard the familiar voice say, removing all doubt. "You look positively quanked. Were you intentionally trying to blow yourself up?"

"Quanked? Did you make that up? Sounds like it has something to do with ducks."

"Overpowered by fatigue," she answered. "Although you appear to have been overpowered by explosions."

"The triggers were percussive, not explosive," I said, echoing Monty's words. "Shit—Monty. Is he okay?"

Karma looked across the courtyard. "He's still alive. Some broken bits, but that's bound to happen when you slam yourself into a wall at that speed."

"He didn't slam himself, I slammed him."

"I know. I just wanted to make sure you were aware of the consequences of your actions."

I tried sitting up, but my body and the arrow impaling me were vetoing that move, so I opted for propping myself on my elbows, at least until Earth got its axis under control. Karma stood next to me and placed Grim Whisper on the ground near my hand. The blood-arrow wound in my shoulder throbbed with every heartbeat.

"What happened? You're late."

"Late?" she said, raising an eyebrow with a mix of curiosity and menace only she could pull off. "Late for what?"

She was dressed in an upscale version of the Kuro Hyogikai: black suit, white shirt, no sword. On her left lapel I saw the red, stylized B. Her loose hair framed her face, giving her a younger appearance. I didn't know how old she was, but I imagined if she counted birthdays, it was in eons. She looked down at me with an expression of disapproval mixed with amazement.

Karma. Actually, the irony wasn't lost on me in the moment.

"Late," I said, suicidally. "As in, not here on time. I pressed the mark."

She looked around and took in the devastation and damage.

"I noticed. You do realize Kali's mark is not a summoning rune?"

"I do," I said. "It's just that they...I couldn't stop them. They dropped that net on Peaches...I wasn't thinking...then I pressed the mark."

"In a courtyard full of runic triggers."

"And where were you?" I asked, continuing to take my life into my own hands. "Busy? Is that why you were late?"

She crouched down and wrapped her delicate fingers around the lower half of my face, cupping my chin. For anyone else, this would have been a gentle caress of tenderness. For her, it was like having my face in a vise.

"I am *never* late, Splinter," she said, applying a small amount of pressure. "Karma is always on time. I am cause and effect and ever present."

I knew it was a gentle amount of pressure because I only blacked out for a second or two, and when she slapped me back to consciousness, I still had all my teeth.

"They took Peaches," I said, rubbing my face and moving my jaw slowly. "They took him."

"Yes, they did," she said. "You have something they want. The real question is: are you going to give it to them?"

My body was still blazing as it dealt with the injuries. My brain functions were returning to normal, but emotions have a tendency to cloud even the wisest among us. In that moment, the anger and anxiety I felt was slowly mixing into rage. Not the white-hot kind, no, this was more of the slow burn of laying waste to an entire city until I felt satisfied.

That would only happen when I got Peaches back.

"Of course," I said my voice low and full of menace. "Right after I put Esti and her psychohunters in the ground."

"That may be difficult with a blood arrow in your shoulder," she said, pointing at my arm. "Those arrows are a nasty piece of work. Looks like this Esti is a bit angry with you."

"Something like that. She wants the blood blades back, blames me for killing her leader, and wants Chi and me dead."

"Are they valid?" Karma asked. "The things she blames you for?"

"I didn't steal the blades, I'm not a vampire." I paused for a second "But I did kill her leader, yes. Now I have to finish the job."

"You make the most interesting friends, Splinter," Karma said. "I take it you will not comply with their requests for your or the vampire's demise."

"Correct," I said. "Why didn't you come right *after* I pressed the mark? Not that I was summoning you."

"That's a conversation for another time," she said. "You have more pressing matters. We will talk later, if you manage to remain among the living."

"Can you help me find Peaches?" I asked, knowing the answer. "Or, at least point me in the right direction?"

"That would be overextending my influence, not to mention skewing things in ways that would only cause you immense amounts of pain later. I'm sorry, but I won't subject you to that."

"Life is pain," I said, nodding. "In that case, think you can give me an assist with the arrow?"

She smiled knowingly at me. I hadn't directly tried to manipulate her: that would be a slappable offense. I really wanted her help, but knowing how she had reacted in the past, my face wasn't resilient enough to take any more of her slaps.

"Well played, Splinter."

I knew better than to ask for her direct help in finding Peaches. As the embodiment of causality, I knew she would say no. But I tried the big ask first, remembering how bad blood arrows were and hoping she would at least minimize some of the exploding.

"Which would you prefer? Dealing with the explosive arrow, or dealing with the explosive body? I won't do both."

"Explosive arrow," I said. "I've had enough mind-numbing

pain to last me a long time. I'd like to avoid exploding parts of my body."

"Very well," she said and placed a hand on my arm, grabbing the arrow with the other hand. Blood Hunters used broadhead arrows, which meant the retraction was going to rate a twenty on the ten-point agony scale. "Are you ready?"

"No," I said. "Wouldn't it be better to push it through?"

"Ordinarily, yes, but the more blood it contacts, the greater the chance of explosion—for you," she answered, her voice grim. "Do you regrow limbs?"

"Can we not find out today?"

"Fair enough. Ready?"

"Pull it out," I said, bracing myself. "I'll deal with the arrow if you give me a moment to heal."

"You are currently in stasis. Once I leave—well, I suggest you don't hold on to the arrow after that."

What made these arrows so dangerous was their delayed explosive quality. Once the runes came in contact with blood, they converted the blood around the wound into a liquid explosive similar to nitromethane mixed with ammonium nitrate.

It meant that not only was the arrow explosive, but the target became a ticking time bomb themselves. I didn't know what would happen if my arm blew off, and I wasn't in the mood to test that aspect of my curse today.

"I'm ready," I said after a few seconds. "Do it."

Karma pulled out the arrow and white-hot pain blossomed in my shoulder. It felt like my arm had burst into flame as I groaned and nearly lost consciousness. I looked over at my shoulder and expected it to be barbecued beyond saving, but it was only bruised and bloody.

"Your body should be able to repair itself now," she said. "Now, the tainted blood."

"Wait, what do you mean tainted—?"

I barely managed the words before she plunged two fingers into the wound without warning. The pain blinded me; I bit down until I tasted blood, my vision tunneling in as she dug in my shoulder for what felt like an eternity. I could feel myself slipping into shock.

The next thing I felt was her light slap bringing me back into sharp clarity. It felt like getting hit softly with a hammer. In her hand, she held a blood-soaked arrow covered in a small cloud of black energy.

"That it?" I asked, feeling better by the second as my body dealt with the damage. "Any more surprise blood removal?"

"It's all there," she said, looking at the arrow in her hand. "I suggest you dispose of this immediately after I leave."

"Off to dispense some more of yourself?"

"I like to think of myself as being the just reward for people," Karma said. "Good or bad—especially bad."

"Like a vigilante bitch," I said. "I mean that in the best way possible."

Karma nodded with a smile as red and black energy crackled around her body.

"A bitchilante, yes. I approve," she said, handing me the arrow. "You have ten seconds after I leave."

"Thank you for the karmically imbued slaps of clarity," I said, slowly getting to my feet and rubbing my jaw. "I'll be feeling them for a while."

"They aren't as potent as hellhound saliva," she said with a tight smile. "But it is my position that stupidity should hurt."

Then she disappeared.

EIGHTEEN

Ten seconds doesn't feel like a long time.

It's all a matter of context. Holding your breath for ten seconds—easy. Holding your hand in a blazing open furnace for ten seconds—not so easy. Holding an explosive arrow and getting it far enough away from you, while protecting your unconscious partner, who was probably in the blast radius, in ten seconds—complicated.

I couldn't just throw it in any direction. The courtyard was large, but I didn't know if it was large enough to offset the triggers that hadn't detonated. I set my mental clock to ten seconds, threw the arrow to the end of the courtyard I'd cratered with my body and ran toward Monty's prone form.

I didn't want to take the chance of activating more triggers. and so only pressed the main bead on my bracelet, materializing my shield. I placed it between us and the arrow, bracing myself against the coming blast.

The arrow exploded, and I crouched closer to Monty. A tsunami of energy crashed into the shield, propelling us out of the courtyard and into the street. My shield stayed mostly intact as we rolled out onto the sidewalk. Monty groaned as I got to my knees, absorbing what remained of the shield.

I looked back into the courtyard and saw a deep trench running through the center of it. The far wall was missing a large section where the arrow had exploded. I took in the damage and realized even with the subtle runes keeping people away, Fumiko wouldn't be too far behind this explosion.

"Next time," I said, crawling over to where Monty lay, "we postpone the overseas trip and stay home."

"You...survived the triggers," Monty said, groggily. "Well done."

"Sure, thanks. We need to get off the street before Fumiko and the bankermages show up."

I got Monty to his feet and we shuffled down the street. One of his arms hung limply by his side, and I could feel him favoring one leg as we limped away from the courtyard.

"They will arrive soon," Monty said, looking around. "The runes won't mask that explosion from the Kuro Hyogikai."

"How bad is it?" I asked, looking down at his arm. "Can you cast?"

"Feels like an ulnar break and tibial shaft fracture at the talus."

"The triggers did that?"

"The wall did that," Monty said, grimacing. "The triggers just facilitated the energy to launch me into the wall. I came away mostly intact, considering their force."

"Can you fix it?"

Monty nodded. "Battlemages learn field medicine as part of their training. These breaks are painful, but don't require a medical facility," he said. "I'd prefer not to cast runes in the middle of the street, though. Sooner or later, someone will stop and investigate."

Surprisingly, Japan was very much like New York City. No one paid us any attention as we stumbled along. We got a few concerned looks, but no one approached us. Then again, we were a ragged, bloody mess, and I wouldn't have approached us either.

"We need a doorway," Monty said, pointing down one of the side streets. "Over there."

"It's probably locked," I said, not understanding why Monty needed a doorway. "Just how hard did you hit that wall?"

"Hard enough to realize we underestimated Esti and the Blood Hunters," Monty answered, leaning against the wall. "They took your creature?"

"Yes," I said after a pause. "I'm sorry I pressed the mark and slammed you into the wall. I wasn't thinking. I saw them throw the lattice over him...and now he's gone."

The side street was hidden in shadow. Monty took a second to catch his breath, gestured over his arm and grimaced. Golden runes fell over his body as he repaired the breaks. Battlemages learned the necessary skills to do what they did best—fight.

"No apologies necessary," Monty said. "As I said, we underestimated Esti and her group."

"Since when do Blood Hunters have sorceresses?" I asked, looking down the side street. "No one mentioned sorceresses. What was that sphere they formed?"

"A nullification sphere," Monty answered, holding up his arm as he tested the handiwork of the golden runes on his body. "Where they learned it is the problem. That is an advanced cast, even for an accomplished sorcerer."

"That's why they didn't get pounded to bits. The sphere neutralized the triggers. How's the arm and leg?"

"Stiff, but serviceable," he said, approaching the door. "It would appear Esti bolstered her numbers with sorcery after our last run-in on Ellis Island. It was a serious, almost lethal miscalculation on my part."

"We need to get him back," I said, letting the rage flow over me. "She's going to hurt him."

"Remember what I told you," Monty said as he began

gesturing and red runes flowed into the door. "It's nearly impossible to hurt a hellhound."

"She said she was going to starve and torture him, Monty."

"For your creature, those are probably one and the same," Monty said, still focusing on the door. "We'll get him back."

"If we don't bring her Chi, she's going to unleash him on the city," I said quietly. "You know what they will do to him if he's let loose on the city in that state."

Monty turned to me. "I know what they will *try* to do, but they will not succeed."

"Didn't they see Wick?" I asked. "Don't they know…you never touch the dog? That rule has to be taken to the nth degree when that dog is *my* hellhound."

"I'm afraid they didn't get that memo," Monty said, grabbing my shoulder. "You have to maintain control. If you become agitated, it will affect your creature. In his weakened state, it could strain your bond."

"Strain the bond?"

"Which could cause his body to repeat what happened in London as a protective defense. Something you want to prevent right now."

"You mean he would go XL? Wouldn't it be easier to find him if he was enormous?"

"Not just for us, but for anyone," Monty said. "Some of whom would attack first and ask questions later."

"The last thing we need right now is a Peaches XL," I said, realizing the truth. "They would just see a monster and try to destroy him."

"The operative word there is *try*," Monty added. "It would be best if we found him and dealt with the Blood Hunters."

"There's only one way to deal with Esti and her group," I said. "First, we need to find Chi."

"Agreed." Monty released one more set of runes before the

entire door flared red for a split second. "Can you feel the bond you share with him?"

I closed my eyes and slowed my breathing. Nothing. The bond that connected me to Peaches was gone.

"I can't. I can't feel anything," I said as the worst case scenarios flashed through my mind. "It's gone. He's gone."

NINETEEN

"Try again," Monty said. "Feel for the bond."

"I just told you—" I started, frustrated.

"Again," Monty said with an edge. "You're letting your worry and anger cloud your ability. Try again."

I closed my eyes and slowed my breath. I pushed all thoughts out of my mind and focused on Peaches. After what felt like a lifetime, I felt the bond. It was tenuous, but it was there.

"I got it," I said, almost whispering, as if raising my voice would sever the connection. "I can barely feel it, but it's there. I can't tell where he is, but I can sense him."

"You don't have enough sensitivity to pick up on the bond," Monty said. "We need to get you a signal boost."

"Can't you—I don't know…do a finger wiggle and hit me with a signal-boosting rune of deep sensing or something?"

"First of all," Monty said, slipping into wikimage mode, "no such rune exists. Second, we need something to boost your inherent ability. It has to be powerful and fast acting."

"Is there something like that?"

"Yes. It's almost impossible to find, highly illegal, and most certainly dangerous."

"Will it work? Will it make me strong enough to find Peaches?"

"Yes, it will, but there are risks. I will try and minimize them, but we are taking a chance going this route."

"If it helps me find Peaches, I'll take all the risks necessary. I can still feel the bond, but it's faint."

"Good," Monty said. "Let go. If you can barely feel it, they must be masking him."

"The lattice?" I asked. "Is that what they're using to hide him?"

"It would be a combination of the lattice and the sphere they cast over him. Let's go."

"Where exactly are we going?" I asked, looking at the door with distrust. "Unless we're entering an armory, I don't see the point of this."

"We need to approach things differently," Monty said.

"By differently, I hope you mean non-explosively," I said. "I've had enough of the blowing up today."

"Esti made a correct assessment," Monty answered, grabbing the door handle. "We were out of our league and out of our depth. Clearly, she has learned how to face us since our last encounter. We need to get equipped."

"Oh, good, this door leads to a battalion of angry mages?"

"Not quite," he said. "You already have one angry battlemage on your side. You don't need a battalion."

"So, what's in here?"

"Opportunity."

He turned the handle of the door. I expected to see the interior of someone's home or business; instead, I was looking down a wide, brightly lit, empty hallway. In the center of the hallway stood a man dressed in standard mageform—upscale black suit, white shirt, and gray tie. That's where the similarities ended. His face was covered by a featureless white mask, giving off a serious Phantom of the Opera vibe.

He held a silver, rune-covered six-foot staff in one hand, a short sword in the other, and both legs sported thigh holsters holding larger versions of Grim Whisper. Around him, softly glowing red orbs moved around his body in lazy orbits.

"Who or what is that?" I asked as Monty entered the hallway. Stepping in behind him, I reflexively paused to let Peaches catch up when I remembered. A fresh pang of anger and grief squeezed my heart as I closed the door behind us. "Since when do mages carry an arsenal?"

"That is not a mage," Monty said. "That is one of the Janus—a Doorman."

"Dresses like a mage, uses a staff like a wizard, and has dual pistols—a magizard gunslinger?"

"No, a Doorman. The Janus are gatekeepers. Powerful gatekeepers."

"He doesn't look like any doorman I've ever seen," I said, looking around and noticing the door behind us had vanished. "Tell me you don't have to fight him."

"Doormen guard the emergency exits and entrances to certain locations," Monty answered. "This is the Janus to the Moving Market."

"Moving Market as in Shadow Nick's Moving Market?" I asked. "I thought it would be shut down after his death."

"The Moving Market is too important to be closed because of any one person. It is currently under new management: Director Tessa Wract."

Every community has a dark side—the face that's kept hidden from the light, and from outsiders. It's revealed in the shadows, when you're out of options or looking to erase any trace. It's the corner of dark alleys, whispers of promised vengeance, the impact of a life-ending round between your eyes, or a soul-stealing rune turning your body cold and lifeless before it hits the ground.

The magical community was no exception, its dark side was only more dangerous because of the forces involved. The Moving

Market dealt in lethality and the lost—and those wishing to remain that way. If you wanted to disappear, you slid into the Market. If you were taken there—the end result was the same. You were gone.

Most of the items sold in the Market qualified as contraband: something to disintegrate a target on sight, a rune to control a person's mind, or information you needed to destroy a rival. You could find it all in the Moving Market—for a price.

"Mage Montague, you have requested emergency access to the Moving Market," the Janus said, his voice reverberating in the hallway. "Identification, please."

"Of course." Monty stepped close and stared at the mask. A golden light emanated from his eyes as the Janus nodded.

"Tristan Montague, mage of the Golden Circle. Identification confirmed. You and your guest may proceed."

The Doorman stepped to one side and let us pass. At the other end of the corridor, behind the Janus, I saw a large rune-covered door.

"What happens if you have the wrong ID?"

"No one has ever gotten into the Moving Market without authorization," Monty said, glancing back at the Janus. "There is no recorded instance of a Doorman being defeated while guarding a door. I've wondered if it's even possible."

"I'm really glad we didn't have to find out if it was," I said, glancing back at the Janus. "He looks pretty high up in the 'dispensing of an ass-whooping' category."

"I'd say that is a fair assessment of his abilities," Monty said, placing a hand on the door and pushing. "Remember the law of the Market and keep your wits about you."

TWENTY

We stood in Market Central.

They had made significant changes since the last time I was here. The entire market was arranged like a wheel formed of seven concentric circles. This building, which also doubled as the main base of operations, acted as the hub of the wheel. The rings were arranged in order of influence and power.

The higher ranked magic-users inhabited the rings closest to the hub. The two outer rings were a no-man's land and dead zone. If you found yourself on an outer ring, it was only a matter of time before someone or something tried to introduce you to the concept of dead zone—emphasis on dead.

There was only one law in the Market: only the strong, cunning, or ruthless survived for any length of time. After losing Peaches, I was feeling particularly homicidal and made sure everyone around me felt the intention of my thoughts.

We stood in a large reception area that resembled the lobby of a large hotel.

"We need to see the new director before we get outfitted," Monty said, waiting. "It should be any moment."

ORLANDO SANCHEZ

"Who is this new Director Tessa Wract?" I asked, looking around. "Is she a plane-weaver like Nick?"

Plane-weavers could travel between planes with ease, allowing them to go literally anywhere with a thought. Nick took this a step further and transported a city block with him. He was good at what he did until he made the wrong enemies, got in over his head, and lost it—literally.

"No," Monty said, moving to the reception area. "Tessa is a mage with a focus on temporal discipline. A time-weaver. One of a handful, and the most powerful in time manipulation."

"Time-weaver?" I asked. "Is that a plane-weaver in a hurry?"

"You'd better let me do the talking," Monty answered. " A time-weaver like Tessa dwarfs Nick's abilities and power by several orders of magnitude. She keeps the Moving Market... moving. Not only does she slip it in-between planes, she's also powerful enough to move it through time. Her first, second, and only concern after herself is the Market—remember that."

"Got it, scary lady mage with time powers, don't piss her off right away."

"Don't piss her off...at all," Monty said with a sigh. "The Moving Market, despite its appearance, is hostile territory. Treat it as such."

"Monty, she moves a building around through spacetime. Isn't that what Professor Ziller does? I don't hear you describing him as the Zillerbogeyman."

"Before Tessa was assigned to running the Market, she'd had some unpleasant run-ins with mages working for the Dark Council."

"I'm liking her already."

"Tessa was considered an elder of the Dark Council," Monty continued. "The last incident caused them to expel her from the Council."

"Now I'm really liking her," I said. "She got herself kicked out of the Council? For what?"

116

"The rumors were that she had temporally stranded a mage in a conscious time loop," Monty said. "This was a mage much like someone I know who couldn't control his verbal outbursts."

"Don't know who you're talking about," I said. "Restraint is my new name, remember?"

"The mage went too far and ended up insulting her," Monty said, his voice serious. "She placed him in a contained interstitial time loop and forced the mage to repeat the same thirty seconds of his castration over and over."

"Oh, fuck," I said under my breath. "Are you serious?"

Monty nodded. "She kept him there until he went mad, and only then, when she was certain he could no longer be aware of the torture, did she kill him. After that, they offered her an option—erasure, or the Moving Market."

"She willingly chose the Market and you want to do business with this Tessa?"

"We are out of options at this point," Monty answered. "She carries what we need to be able to effectively deal with Esti and her hunters."

"She sounds *worse* than Esti. You sure this is our *only* option?"

"Yes. Remember what I said: hostile territory. She is not our friend, and even sharks smile before they rip you to shreds."

"Wonderful. Are there any mages you know who aren't skirting the edge of insanity?"

"Of course," Monty said, brushing off the sleeves of his ruined suit. "Plenty of mages have chosen to live a life of quiet solitude and study, perfecting their craft."

"Where are those mages? Because every mage or energy manipulator I've met so far has been on the far end of unstable."

"We are, by definition, an unstable group," Monty said. "I could be living quietly in the Golden Circle, but I'm in New York City, working with a detective who is bonded to a hellhound, cursed alive by an angry goddess, somehow entwined with an ancient vampire, and who is currently being pursued by a group of vampire killers led by a deranged, vengeance-driven psychopath—that sounds like the definition of stability."

"When you put it that way—" I started as a short woman holding a clipboard approached us. She was dressed in a casual business suit and her name-tag read 'Kathy.'

"Welcome, Mage Montague," Kathy said. "This way, please. Ms. Wract is waiting for you."

TWENTY-ONE

K athy led us to the other end of the reception area.

The space was done in minimalist art deco, with plenty of wood and stone surrounding the open area in the center. The subtle smell of citrus and fresh earth made me pause for a second until I noticed the vases filled with flowers on several of the wall stands.

Standing in the reception area surrounded by several women dressed like Kathy, and fielding questions in rapid-fire fashion, stood who I could only assume was Tessa. She smiled when she saw us, motioning for Kathy to approach. She turned to the circle of assistants around her and, with a word, dispatched them.

Tessa wore a black Armani pantsuit, which made her white hair seem to glow. She commanded the attention of those around her with a sense of ease and a subtle undercurrent of menace. She was slightly taller than I expected, standing nearly my height. She gave me a pleasant smile, and I remembered Monty's words: *even sharks smile before they rip you to shreds.* Her piercing hazel eyes shimmered with violet power as we approached with Kathy in the lead.

"Tristan Montague," she said, her smile transforming to a

tight scowl a second later as she gave Monty a disapproving shake of her head. "What kind of fashion statement is this? Nouveau bomb victim?" She turned. "Kathy, is it?"

"Yes, ma'am?" Kathy answered as if she had been jolted.

"We do not allow our guests to wander the premises looking like victims of an explosion—even if they *were* victims of an explosion. Please have a set of clothing sorted for each."

"Yes, ma'am, right away."

"Oh, and Kathy?" Tessa added as the woman started moving away rapidly.

Kathy stopped in her tracks as if nailed to the floor. The actual maneuver was quite impressive—whatever material the soles of her shoes were made out of must have possessed traction beyond belief.

"Yes, ma'am?" Kathy asked with a slight quiver in her voice. "Anything else, ma'am?"

"Don't let this happen again," Tessa said, allowing some of her energy to fill the reception area. The surge of power made everyone around us immediately step away. "Do I make myself clear?"

"Absolutely, ma'am," Kathy said, her face ashen. The tremor in the clipboard she held matched the shakiness in her voice. "It won't happen again."

"Good. We'll be in my office. Have the clothes delivered to the guest suite."

"Monty," I muttered. "Maybe this is a mistake."

"Mr. Strong," Tessa said. "There are no mistakes or coincidences. You are here because you are meant to be here. Come."

TWENTY-TWO

We left the reception area as Tessa placed a hand on the wall.

A section slid back and we entered her office. Tessa's office was a large, expansive area. Neat stacks of paper covered her behemoth Parnian desk, and set in front of it were two large leather chairs. The walls were bare, except for a large reproduction of Dali's *The Persistence of Memory*. A smaller version of the same work sat on her desk.

"Is that the original?" I asked, pointing at the smaller version. "I thought it was in a museum?"

"You have a discerning eye, Mr. Strong," Tessa said, sitting behind her desk. "That's the original. Salva is a good friend and extended me this courtesy."

"But he painted this in 1931," I said, confused. "Are you saying you went back and had him—?"

"Like I said," she said with a smile that didn't quite reach her eyes. "Salva is a good friend. Please sit."

I sat in one of the two large chairs facing her. Monty sat in the other. Upon closer inspection, I realized I was sitting in a Gio Ponti 1950's armchair. Next to her behemoth of a desk stood another assistant though this one was dressed differently than Kathy and the crew outside. She wore a pantsuit almost identical to Tessa's. She also held a large tablet and wore an earpiece.

"This is my personal assistant, Eileen," Tessa said, motioning to the woman. "She will be taking your requisition."

"Thank you, Tessa," Monty said. "I apologize for the inconvenience."

"You used an emergency locator, and from the looks of your suit, it *was* an emergency. Was that a runed Zegna?"

"It was," Monty said, glancing down at what remained of his suit. "We encountered an overly prepared adversary while being unprepared ourselves."

"How is Japan?" Tessa said, sitting back in her chair. "I hear the Blood Hunters are roaming the streets. This have anything to do with you two?"

"How did you—?" I started.

"Do you know what the most valuable item in the Moving Market is, Mr. Strong?"

"Information," I said. "It can open doors that nothing else can open."

She narrowed her eyes at me and nodded.

"Correct," she said. "Tristan operated the emergency rune sequence from Osaka. We recently heard of a minor disturbance involving Blood Hunters, two unidentified males, and a"—she looked at Eileen, who looked down at her tablet—"what was it?"

"A dog of undetermined origin," Eileen said, reading off her tablet. "Accounts are unclear what breed it was, and no photographic evidence exists as of this moment. We will check in with the tech department later."

"That sound familiar?" Tessa asked. "Did you see a strange dog out there while fighting the Blood Hunters?"

I figured this was a test—Tessa didn't seem like the kind to ask a question she didn't have the answer to. Plus, if I lied to her,

I had a feeling it would make getting what we needed from her harder.

I glanced at Monty, who nodded, disguising it in a short cough.

"Excuse me," he said. "Would you happen to have some tea?"

"Of course," Tessa replied. "Eileen, Earl Grey for Tristan, properly steeped, and Deathwish for Mr. Strong—the extra death version."

Eileen pressed the surface of the tablet and nodded.

"Your beverages will be here shortly," Eileen said.

"Well, Mr. Strong?" Tessa asked again. "Strange breed of dog?"

"Yes," I said. "That strange breed is my hellhound, Peaches."

Tessa looked at Eileen who quietly left the room.

"Thank you for your candor," Tessa said. "Do the Blood Hunters know they have captured a hellhound?"

"Yes," I said. "They took him to make a trade."

"A trade? Really? What do they want for the hellhound? What do you have?"

"They want my blade, and a particular vampire I know."

"Michiko Nakatomi," Tessa answered. "Recently arrived in Japan. Last known whereabouts, Hokkaido. May I see the blade?"

I unsheathed Ebonsoul and placed it on her desk.

"You don't want to get cut by it."

"I would imagine not," Tessa said, admiring Ebonsoul. "And Ms. Nakatomi gave you this?"

"She did, along with the death threats that are part of the package."

"This is what a god-killer looks like," Tessa said, not touching it. "And it's a seraph? How did you manage that?"

"You tell me," I said, semi-frustrated and completely surprised she could know so much. "You seem to be incredibly well-informed."

"Touché," she said with a smile. "As you said, information demands the highest price. What do you need, Tristan?"

"Daystrider armor, entropy rounds, and safe passage in and out of the seventh ring," Monty said. "I need to speak to *him*."

"Are you mad?" Tessa asked. "Were you in the center of the explosion?"

"I would imagine the Director of the Moving Market has absolute control," Monty said, leaning back. "Was I mistaken?"

"Do not pretend to goad me, Tristan," Tessa said, her voice laced with anger. "Daystrider armor and entropy rounds are child's play. I have no love for the Blood Hunters. Consider their acquisition a gift, courtesy of the Market."

"The seventh ring?"

"Is suicide, Tristan," Tessa snapped. "I will not be the one to explain to your uncle why you are a pile of bloody dust. No."

"I need to meet with Roque."

Tessa stared at Monty for close to twenty seconds before letting out a sigh.

"I see," Tessa said. "You've come to the Moving Market to die."

"Not if I can help it," Monty said. "He has what we need."

"What you need is to get out of my Market before I have you forcibly ejected," Tessa said. "Roque will kill you as soon as he lays eyes on you. What could he possibly have that I can't provide?"

"Dragon's blood," Monty said quietly. "We need it. He has it."

"I don't know where you heard—" Tessa started, holding up a hand.

"Don't," Monty said, his voice slicing through the quiet office. "Do not lie to me."

"Tristan," Tessa said. "Have you gone dark? You know the dangers of dragon's blood. You know how volatile it is."

"It's not for me," Monty said, glancing at me. "It's for him."

"Are you trying to kill him?" Tessa almost yelled. "I don't care if he's the 'Chosen of Kali' and every other goddess in creation. Dragon's blood will end him."

"Safe passage in and out of the seventh ring," Monty said, undeterred. "And a meeting with Roque, by tonight."

I could see Tessa get herself under control in stages. She finally managed to let out a deep breath, then rested both arms on her chair and steepled her fingers.

"Very well," Tessa said. "I will send the word. I will also inform your uncle of this madness."

"Feel free to do as you wish," Monty said.

"I'm so pleased I have your permission. You need to rethink this. Going to see him will end badly—for you."

"Please let me know the cost of the armor, the ammunition, and the arrangement."

"The armor and ammunition is a gift. The arrangement may be more than either of you can afford."

Eileen came back with the coffee and tea. Monty grabbed the cup of Earl Grey and held the tray out in front of me.

"No sense refusing our host's excellent hospitality," he said, moving the tray in front of me until I took the cup of Deathwish. "Thank you again, Tessa."

Tessa scowled and placed a hand on her desk. A section glowed violet, and then across the office, the exit opened.

"Don't thank me," she snapped. "Now, get out while I arrange your funeral."

Monty raised his cup in her direction and headed out of the office and into the reception area. I turned and saw a fuming Tessa.

"Thank you, I guess?" I said, holding up the mug of Deathwish. "I appreciate the help, really, and this coffee...excellent."

Tessa's eyes glowed violet as she stared at me.

"Get out...now."

I followed Monty out of the office before she decided to help by blasting me out of existence.

TWENTY-THREE

"What did you just do?" I asked, catching up to Monty. "She is pissed."

"Not here," Monty said in between sips. "Too exposed."

We left the reception area and headed out another door into the street. Behind us, I could see some of the women dressed like Kathy trying to hover close to us. I imagined they had been given instructions to eavesdrop or at the very least keep an eye on us.

The main hub of the Market reminded me of the Village in New York. It was made up of small streets that criss-crossed one another with no rhyme or reason or suddenly ended without warning. Most people thought the Village was quaint, giving the city an old-world feel. I preferred to think of it as a maze of infernal design.

"We need to lose them," I said, walking down the street. "They wouldn't be following us if we had Peaches."

"I think they'd fear Tessa more than your hellhound." He pointed. "Over there—they won't follow us inside."

Since we were in the main hub, this part of the Market also housed the most upscale stores with the most expensive and exotic items. Monty entered a small bookstore named, *Accursed*

Verse, which reminded me of every old bookstore I had spent some time in. Cramped aisles brimming with books made up the bulk of the store, and at its front they had created a special display labeled *First Editions.*

The musty smell of paper mixed with the scent of coffee gave me a feeling of literary comfort and familiarity. I had the overwhelming desire to take the books with me—all of the books. Monty traced a rune, and the feeling of getting books immediately subsided.

As we passed the entrance and front display, I read some of the titles and realized I was looking at first editions of some of the most well-known books in history.

"Are the books up front all—?"

"Yes," Monty said with an appraising nod. "First editions in pristine condition."

"And they sell them for how much?" I asked, looking around in awe. "This is a fortune in books."

"Tessa charges a small fortune for each," Monty answered, his expression dark. "Exorbitant is the starting price point."

"If people buy them knowing the price is inflated, it's not her fault. It's like paying three thousand dollars for the full experience of Tieguanyin. It's just oolong tea."

"I have no issue with a free market system, but we are not in a 'free market' here."

"What's the issue, then?" I asked. "The books explode?"

"The problem is that the current owner of a recently purchased book from this shop never lasts long enough to enjoy their purchase," Monty answered, leading us to the back rows where the books didn't seem as interesting.

"Excuse me? Are you saying Tessa goes out and eliminates the customers?"

"No," Monty said, gesturing. "It's nothing as sinister as that. All of the books in this shop are cursed."

"Oh, that's all?" I said, stepping away from the shelves. "The books are cursed?"

"Yes. You felt the first part, the desire to take them with you," Monty said, running a finger down a spine. "Some say these books are almost sentient."

"Taking books home isn't a curse. You like reading, but these books aren't calling out to you."

"We are currently standing in the philatelic section."

"This is the porn section?" I said, looking around and trying to glance at the titles without really looking at them. Some of the titles made me wonder. *Don't Lick Them* sat next to *Stamp It Like You Mean It!*, which sat next to *Squeeze it Gently—A Guide to Expert Tweezing*.

"I said philatelic, not fellat—nevermind. In any case, even in this section of *stamp collecting* they exert a pull. I make it a point to avoid the magical tome and grimoire section."

"Oh, stamp collecting…are you sure? Some of these titles… Just saying," I said. "And *all* the books are cursed?"

"Yes, it's a gradual escalation curse. First, things start breaking around the house, items go missing—then it moves on to physical harm."

"Physical harm? Really?"

"Yes. It'll start with something innocuous, like a stubbed toe. Then it will proceed to something more serious like spilling boiling water, or a semi-serious cut while preparing food."

"Does it get worse?"

"I would assume so, but no one has kept a book long enough to find out. The books are paid for, and if you want to return one, you need to pay a refund fee to have the books removed from your home."

"Let me get this straight, you buy the book, and then you have to pay a fee to have the book removed?"

"Only if you want the curse lifted," Monty said. "Imagine a

book from this store used as a weapon. Send someone you don't like a book from here and—"

"That's wrong on so many levels," I said. "Can't we do anything?"

"Right now we have bigger problems to deal with," Monty said with one last gesture. "There—we have some privacy."

He had created a sphere of silence around us. The air around me grew pressurized, and my ears popped as I forced a yawn to regulate the pressure in my head.

"Let's start with who this Rocky is," I said. "He sounds dangerous. Why does he want to kill you?"

"Roque. He *is* dangerous," Monty said. "He was a Golden Circle mage who had his abilities erased by the elders of the Circle for the abuse and usage of blood magic to take a life. It was actually many lives."

"Why does he hate you? You were never an elder."

"I wasn't, but my father and uncle both were," Monty said. "They were the ones who erased him."

"So what's the issue? He has no abilities," I said. "How can he hurt you?"

"He reacquired his abilities, but something was wrong. They had mutated somehow—he had mutated."

"He's a mutant?"

"I didn't say *he* was a mutant, only that he changed after the erasure."

"What happened to him? Why is he in the Moving Market?"

"He managed to find a natural source of drake's blood," Monty said. "I don't know where or how. He drank the blood and undid the erasure, but the blood was too potent. His body couldn't withstand the infusion of power. It destroyed him and altered his mind, driving him insane."

"No wonder he wants to kill you," I said. "He blames your family."

"Yes, he does. But we aren't going to see him."

"You told Tessa you needed to meet with him," I said. "We aren't?"

"Are you insane? He's a mage who wants nothing more than to destroy the Montagues. Of course we aren't going to meet him —we just need the dragon's blood."

"Without seeing him?"

"If we can help it," Monty said. "Tessa sending out the word will set things in motion and give us a window of opportunity."

"Why is he in the Moving Market? Why isn't he in some cell or at the Golden Circle?"

"The Market gives him freedom," Monty said. "He inhabits part of the seventh ring and is left alone. Outside of the Market, he would be hunted and killed. I doubt any cell could hold him for long."

"I'm not drinking dragon's blood," I said, quickly. "That stuff sounds beyond dangerous. I'm going to pass."

"Do you want to get your creature back?"

"Of course I want to get Peaches back. You know this."

"Dragon's blood can help us do that, and stop the Blood Hunters."

"That sounds too good to be true," I said. "What's the catch?"

"There is no 'catch.' You have to drink the blood."

"I'm not drinking dragon's blood," I said. "Tessa was right. You've lost your mind."

"The dragon's blood, in minute doses, can enhance the magical ability of the subject. Roque's error was greed—he drank too much too soon, and it undid him."

"No one else has this dragon's blood?" I asked. "I mean, we're in the Moving Market. They have everything...this is the equivalent of an illegal, magical, Wal-Mart, complete with the lethal 'blow your enemies away' sections."

"They don't just *carry* dragon's blood," Monty replied. "No one does, due to its danger and volatility."

"But Rocky does?"

"*Roake* or *Row-kay*," Monty emphasized the name phonetically. "If you ever meet him, do not call him 'Rocky'—and yes, he keeps large quantities of it."

"Synthesize it. Has that been tried?"

"With less than optimal results. Everyone who drank synthetic dragon's blood went blind the first few days right before trying to kill anyone who approached. The last phase of synthetic consumption...the subject would lose all sense of reality and tragically take their own lives."

"This is not encouraging me in the least."

"The natural blood has no such side effects."

"As long as it's taken in small doses," I said, hating this idea. "Do you know how much is too much?"

"Not exactly," Monty answered. "But I know who does."

"Rocky?"

"Yes, and don't call him that."

"Why was Tessa worried about Dex?" I asked. "She came across as all menacey until you brought up the meeting with Rocky."

"She's still menacey—a menace, and dangerous, not to mention incredibly powerful."

"But?"

"My uncle wasn't always as calm as he is now," Monty said. "Especially in fringe populations like the Moving Market, my uncle is well-known."

"He's famous with the criminal element? Dex, really?"

"Closer to infamous and feared. There are several reasons he needed to leave the Golden Circle," Monty said. "His associations with the Ten and other shadow figures made it difficult to put him in a position of authority."

"So, he decided to cut loose?"

"More like he decided to spare the family further ignominy. He made a clean break when he started seeing the Morrigan."

"Makes sense," I said. "Nothing like dating the Chooser of the

Slain to ding your respectability image and scare everyone shitless."

"By that point, the elders feared him and he had had enough. Stepping away was the best thing he could have done."

"He must hate being there now, then."

"Agreed," Monty said with a nod. "I'm sure he is busy trying to find a replacement."

"That would explain Tessa's reaction. She may be strong, but Dex is stronger and his girlfriend is a super scary goddess."

"I'd say that's an apt summation. In any case, she should comply with my request about the meeting, but she will try to protect herself in some way."

"Protect herself?"

"If something happens to us, she will set it up so that it appears to be our fault."

"Ah, plausible deniability," I said. "That way she can wash her hands of us."

"Exactly. I wouldn't put it past her to notify Fumiko and the Kuro Hyogikai about our involvement in the incident this morning."

"That would put Peaches in danger," I said. "Fumiko was already tetchy about him. If she thinks he can be let loose and destroy her city—"

"Yes, I wouldn't put it past Tessa to conveniently share that information if it means she can extricate herself from the situation."

"Then if something happens she can point elsewhere when Dex or anyone comes asking," I said. "She is cunning."

"You don't get to be the Director of the Moving Market by accident. I have a feeling she will try to sabotage our meeting with Roque as well—be wary."

"Why would she want to do that?"

"If Roque kills us, she can say she warned us and is saddened by our deaths, but we didn't listen," Monty said. "Remember, she only cares about two things."

"Herself and the Market."

"Everything and everyone else is expendable in her mind," Monty said, collapsing the sphere. "We need to go."

TWENTY-FOUR

Travel between the rings was managed through transportation passages.

The system was similar to the subway, but shorter, with automated open-air rail cars that could go from ring to ring. Each station between rings one through five required a stop at a checkpoint. From ring five to six, the tunnel was sealed, with a large blast door that only opened with authorization and a travel pass.

Getting to ring seven was going to be a little different. Monty opened the door to Accursed Verse and stepped outside. The street in front of the bookstore was deserted.

"That's odd," Monty said, mostly to himself. "This area of the Market is usually one of the busiest. Where is everyone?"

"I think I found out who's scaring away all of the business." I pointed to the corner across the street. "You think he's here for us?"

Standing there in all his mysterious glory was the Doorman: white mask, silver staff in hand, large sword resting on his back, and enormous guns on his thighs. The red orbs were missing; I figured he was trying to be subtle and blend in.

"It would seem Tessa is sending us an escort to the seventh ring," Monty said as the Doorman approached. "This may complicate things."

"Because things were so simple until now. If you wanted to mess up someone's meeting with a scary mage, how would you do it?"

"I'd send an overpowered gatekeeper under the guise of protection and escort, then have him attack the mage, completely destroying any chance of a peaceful meeting."

"Then, you could even have the 'protection' attack all parties involved in an effort to keep the delicate peace."

"If this happens on the seventh ring, there will be no witnesses."

"Read my mind," I said. "We operate on the premise that everyone is an enemy, then."

"Only way to stay alive in the Market," Monty said, "is to assume that everyone you meet would prefer you dead."

"Have I mentioned how much I dislike this place?"

"Yes," Monty said. "Let's get what we need and exit the Market. I'm pretty certain we have worn out our welcome."

"That's what you get when you piss off the director of the place. Are you sure you know what diplomacy means? I get the feeling you keep using that word, despite not knowing what it means."

The Doorman approached us. He carried a black, medium-sized, Zero Haliburton carbon-fiber travel case. He placed it on the ground in front of us when he got close.

"The Director has provided a change of clothes, Daystrider armor to be worn beneath, and ammunition for your weapon. Since haste is required, I have been instructed to take you to the nearest lodgings to facilitate this change."

"Which are located where?" Monty asked.

The Doorman pointed down the street and started walking. I picked up the case as we followed him.

"That's convenient," I said under my breath. "It's not like they're keeping tabs on us or anything."

"Hostile territory, remember."

"Do you think we can lose him? We're out in the street, not a hallway. Maybe being outside weakens them?"

"Let's get out of these ruined clothes, then we can discuss how to not anger a Janus."

"Ruined?" I said, looking down at my torn and bloody clothes. "I don't know. I prefer 'not so gently' used."

Monty didn't answer as we entered a large building behind the Doorman. The floor was done in alternating brown and white marble tile, resembling a large chessboard. At the far end, behind an immense, rune-covered brass desk with wooden accents, sat a woman. The walls were a rich mahogany that held brass sconces every few feet. On the wall behind the woman, I saw more brass motifs of runic symbols I couldn't make out.

The Doorman walked up to the desk, extended a hand, and waited. She silently handed him a small blue crystal with a nod. He returned the nod and passed the crystal to Monty.

"You may use the room at the end of the corridor. Please utilize your time wisely."

Monty placed the crystal in a special receptacle on the door. The crystal vanished from sight and the door opened with a click. A short hallway led to a large living room. Off to the side, another short corridor must have led to more rooms. A large table sat next to the entrance, and I placed the travel case there.

"This is pretty upscale," I said, taking in the room. "If we ever get time, we could vacation in the Market. I'm pretty sure Roxanne would love this place."

Monty looked out of the window into a brick wall across a dark alley.

"The view could use some work," Monty said, closing the vertical blinds. "We aren't here to sight-see. Let's check what Tessa sent us."

I looked in the bag. The lightweight Daystrider armor was folded in compact pouches small enough to fit a large pocket. The ammo was in sealed boxes. Entropy rounds were banned pretty much everywhere, and I had started using negation rounds, which weren't much nicer, but saved me the aggravation of dealing with the Dark Council and the NYTF. I grabbed the boxes of ammo—I wasn't feeling nice today.

"She didn't manage to pack a tank in there, did she?" I asked, looking in the bag again as I grabbed a Daystrider pouch, and what I assumed to be my change of clothing. "Something small, like an M1 Abrams?"

"I find it unlikely," Monty said, narrowing his eyes at the contents of the case. "I don't see anything out of the ordinary. Let's get dressed and figure out what to do with our escort."

Monty grabbed the Zegna and headed to one of the back rooms. I did the same. I was out about ten minutes later, and Monty was waiting for me.

"Did you put on the Daystrider armor?" I asked, pulling at my pants leg. "They seem to be a bit snug around the thighs."

"Maybe you need to go on a diet?" Monty asked, reminding me of my constant conversation with Peaches. He must have noticed my expression. "My apologies, I didn't mean to be insensitive. I should have realized that comment—"

"No apologies needed," I said. "I'd rather wear the snug armor and not get pierced by another blood arrow."

"Indeed," he said. "Now, how do we prevent our escort from doing something catastrophic?"

"Send him back to his hallway? Or any hallway?"

"It was a rhetorical question. If Tessa sent him, then she wants to make sure Roque and I meet."

"Considering how this Roque feels about you, it would be easy to arrange a miscommunication, start a violent confrontation, and let the Doorman put us to rest."

"Correct," Monty said. "The question is how to prevent that from happening."

"I know how."

I explained my plan.

TWENTY-FIVE

We headed back to the Doorman.

"You cannot fight him, you know," Monty said in a low voice as we walked back. "In case you were wondering about whether that was a viable option."

"His energy signature is off the charts," I said in the same low voice. "I may be daring, dashing, and debonair, but I'm not self-destructive."

"I think you missed another 'D' word, there."

"Distinguished? Disarming?"

"Delusional."

"You really did miss your calling in comedy. It's not too late, you know."

"This plan of yours," Monty started, "requires precise timing and the agreement of Roque. You do remember the part where I mentioned he lost his mind?"

"Self-preservation is a powerful thing, Mage Montague," I said with a wave of my hand. "Leave this to me."

"We are going to die," Monty said. "Horribly and agonizingly."

"I am to escort you to the seventh ring," the Doorman said. "Please follow me."

"Are we going to use the Ringrail?" I asked as we left the building.

"Yes, the Ringrail is the main method of travel throughout the Moving Market."

"Will we need to stop at checkpoints? I noticed we didn't get travel passes for the trip."

"Due to the nature of the request, emergency travel between the rings has been authorized," the Doorman said. "We will be traveling directly to the seventh ring."

"That sounds interesting," I said, glancing at Monty, who gave me a slight nod. "I didn't know direct routes existed."

"They do." The Doorman led us down the street and to a what looked like a subway station. "For moments such as these."

"What do I call you? The Doorman? Janus? Phantom? Do you even have a name?"

"Doorman will suffice."

"Got it, Big D."

"Big D is not my name," the Doorman answered. "You may call me Doorman or Janus. Not Big D."

"Doorman Janus," I said, thinking. "Even better: DJ. I think that suits you better."

"My name is not—" DJ started.

"Don't waste your energy, Doorman," Monty said with a shake of his head. "He's incorrigible."

I'd like to think DJ glared at me from under his mask, but I had no way of telling.

"After you," I said, pointing to the stairs with a flourish. "Lead the way."

We descended the stairs, and I got ready.

My plan was simple, but untested. We'd board the train, I'd grab Monty, then I'd press my mark, hopefully throwing us both into stasis without calling Karma. One visit from her today was enough to last me a lifetime. We would remove the Doorman from the train and once time snapped back, we would keep going —without our escort.

We arrived at the station, and DJ kept walking to the end of the platform. A steel door covered in red warning runes stopped us from proceeding.

DJ placed his hand on the door, and the runes switched from red to blue. He pulled on the handle, opening the door, and kept walking with us in tow. There was an extension to the station platform, and I saw an open-air rail car waiting for us.

"Please board the car." DJ stood to one side as we got on. "This will take us to the seventh ring."

"I thought these things were automated?" I said to Monty. "Why do we need an escort?"

"That is a good question...Doorman?"

"You requested safe passage in and out of the seventh ring. The Director tasked me to ensure your safety. Neither of you are equipped to deal with the denizens of the outermost ring."

"I feel flattered, insulted, and safer all at once," I said. "Is this the only express train to the seventh ring? Once we get moving, are we going to stop?"

"No," DJ said, raising a hand. "For your safety, please remain seated throughout the trip. This rail car will only stop once we reach the seventh ring. It is the only one of its kind."

I sat down next to Monty.

"Do you know where in the seventh ring Rocky lives?" I said under my breath. "Or are we going to wander around, lost, while Tessa dispatches DJ over here to pound us into little bits of dust?"

"I know where he is. Trust me, Roque will be hard to miss."

"And he's going to give us this dragon blood? I'm asking because I have a feeling Tessa is going to be extra pissed once Phantom is forced to walk to the seventh ring or take a local."

"I will convince him," Monty said, his voice grim. "We do not have the luxury of time."

"Speaking of—once we get moving, we execute Plan Launch the Phantom."

"Launch the Phantom?"

"Exactly...get ready."

The Doorman stood, walked over to the control panel and activated the rail car. We pulled out of the station and began accelerating.

TWENTY-SIX

I stood up and moved closer to the seated Doorman. Monty followed my lead and stood next to me.

"I must insist you both sit down, for your own safety," the Doorman said. "We will be arriving shortly."

I turned as if to sit down, then signaled to Monty, who grabbed my shoulder while I pressed my mark. For a few seconds nothing happened, and I wondered if we had entered some kind of null zone. I looked at my hand and shook it—because as everyone knows, when something is defective, a good whack, followed by a quick shake, always does the job.

"What *are* you doing?" Monty hissed. "Press the mark."

"I did," I said, hissing back. "It's not working. We must be in some kind of null area, or something."

"You broke your mark? How did you manage that?"

"How do you break a mark? That doesn't even make sense."

"Please remain seated," the Doorman said, standing up and turning to us. "This is not safe. You must sit—"

I was still examining my mark when it flashed with white light, nearly blinding me in the process.

"What the hell?" I said, blinking the spots out of my vision. "It's never taken that—"

"Bloody hell," Monty said surprised, as he stood next to me. "We're in a temporal stasis. I've never been in the midst of one like—"

"I'd love to hear the wikimage explanation, but we have no time to admire, seriously."

"How long do we have before the flow of time reverts to normal?"

The Doorman stood frozen near the edge of the rail car. He was pointing to our seats, expecting us to sit down and be safe. We were about to *safely* remove him from the rail car.

"We have ten seconds," I said quickly. "Move Phantom, or we lose this opportunity. If Tessa is a temporary-type mage I'm sure she's wondering what the hell is going on right now, and who's doing it. One guess where she's going to look."

"Temporal, and you're right," Monty said, moving to one side of the Doorman while I stood on the other. "Push."

It was awkward because Monty needed to keep one hand on my shoulder to maintain contact or I figured he'd be ejected out of the stasis. We moved the Doorman off the rail car after a few seconds of grunting.

Everything felt heavier while I was in stasis. Since he was frozen in time, I placed the Doorman at an acute angle to the ground, past his center—compromising and disrupting his balance. Once the flow was reestablished, he would fall forward, buying us extra time. Plus, he deserved it for working with Tessa.

A few seconds later, the flow of time returned and several things happened at once: the rail car shot forward, the Doorman looked around doing his best Wile E. Coyote impression, before face planting, and an explosion rocked the express tunnel, collapsing it behind us.

TWENTY-SEVEN

"What the hell was that?" I asked, looking behind us as the tunnel grew lighter with the explosion. "Did we set something off?"

"That—looks like plausible deniability," Monty answered, narrowing his eyes. "It would seem Tessa is hedging her bets."

"Tessa would collapse the tunnel with us in it?"

Monty looked at me with a 'were you not paying attention this whole time' stare.

"Tessa only cares about two things: Tessa and the Market. Collapsing this tunnel will be a minor disruption of Market business, and she can get rid of us in one fell swoop. She is ruthless and efficient."

"I understand her wanting to crush you," I said, sitting on a bench as the rail car sped down the track. "You pissed her off, and worse—you scared her. I'm pretty sure she's not used to feeling fear."

"I doubt it's a familiar emotion."

"But the Phantom is in here with us."

"Actually, he's back there"—Monty pointed behind us —"probably being buried as we speak."

ORLANDO SANCHEZ

"I didn't do anything to her. Why crush me with you?'

"Guilt by association," Monty replied. "She can't leave witnesses. That would be sloppy."

"Collapsing a tunnel on us is neat?"

"Quite, actually. She gets rid of us heading into the dangerous seventh ring after she warned us not to go. She removes a Janus, which only lends weight to her 'it was too dangerous' argument. The explosion, if we somehow managed to escape it, notifies the entire lethal population of the seventh ring that we are on our way."

"Tessa is one cold bitch," I said. "Remind me to deal with her when this is done."

"*Deal* with her?" Monty asked, raising an eyebrow. "What are you going to do...be extra aggravating?"

"*I* may not be able to do anything personally, but I know a guy. A few guys, actually."

"Let's focus on the task at hand," Monty said, waving my words away. "Thanks to this explosion, Roque and the whole seventh ring will be expecting us. We may have an unwelcoming committee when we arrive."

"Why would this be easy?" I asked, adjusting my holster and checking the sheath holding Ebonsoul. "This day can't end fast enough."

I looked up in time to see a flaming orb sail past.

"Looks like they've seen us." Monty shook out his hands. "No questions, no warnings. Let your weapons do the speaking."

"A mage *conversation*—perfect."

I drew Grim Whisper with one hand and pulled out Ebonsoul with the other. The rail car raced toward the station. After a few seconds, I realized it wasn't slowing down. At the end of the station, a large, steel, blast door in the closed position waited to introduce us to new levels of pain and agony.

"It would seem the rail car has been sabotaged," Monty said, looking at the controls. "The braking mechanism is destroyed."

148

"Sabotaged, really? What gave it away? The fact that we aren't slowing down, or that the blast door that should be open is closed, waiting for us to smash into it?"

"I can try slowing us down, but if I get it wrong, we will sail into the blast door like bullets."

"Monty, I've sailed into enough hard objects today—don't get it wrong."

"Understood," he said, gesturing. "Brace yourself."

TWENTY-EIGHT

Monty managed to slow the rail car enough for us to jump off at the station.

"Jump...now!" Monty yelled as we leapt off the rail car. "Take them down!"

A large group of assorted badness advanced on our position. They appeared to be homeless: dressed in rags, torn clothing, and surrounded by a stench that made me want to stop breathing for a few days.

I saw a few glowing hands in the back—mages. Closer to the front, a group holding a variety of polished weapons acted as a wall of death. They looked like a hot mess, but moved with the coordination and precision of a trained fighting force.

"Their clothes look gently abused, but the weapons look new," I said. "Seems like their priorities are out of whack."

"Who do you think supplies them with plenty of weapons and too little of everything else?"

"Tessa. If she keeps them divided, fighting for scraps, they never organize to become a threat to her."

I counted over thirty of them, with about ten being mages.

"I'll deal with the mages," Monty said. "Do not kill them."

"Are they playing by the same rules?" I asked. "Those weapons look like the 'kill them' variety."

"I thought your new name was Restraint?" Monty said, moving forward. "This would be an excellent time to demonstrate it."

"Fuck," I said under my breath. "I'm going to show restraint, but things are going to get broken. Just so you know."

"'Break, don't kill' is an acceptable philosophy here. Share it freely."

"Is Roque in this group?" I asked, looking among the mages.

"No, he will be waiting for us once we clear this group."

Monty's hands began to glow as he ran forward, muttering words under his breath. I checked Grim Whisper, sheathed Ebonsoul to avoid any fatal accidents, and closed the distance.

I still hadn't switched out to entropy rounds because I was saving them for Esti and the Blood Hunters who had taken Peaches. Persuader rounds were designed to scramble neural networks, making them ideal for dealing with magic-users and normals alike. For mages, it meant no more spell-casting for a good ten minutes.

It also made the target lose control of all bodily functions. It's hard to focus on killing someone when your bowels no longer listen to you and expel, well, everything. I liked to use them exclusively on mages and supernaturals—probably another reason the magic community disliked me.

Monty slipped through the front line with extreme violence as he unleashed orbs of air into their chests, shunting them out of the way. I started picking them off as they got to their feet. It was, I have to say, a shitty thing to do—in more ways than one—but they deserved it for trying to kill us.

Monty unleashed a barrage of red orbs that slammed into our unwelcoming committee of mages. Some of the mages managed to evade and deflect the orbs, closing the distance, and Monty engaged them.

He let them get close and blocked fists and kicks with elbows, knees, hard slaps reminiscent of Karma, throws, and breaks. With a sweep of his hand, a golden shield materialized in front of him, followed by more orbs of air, punching into the mages. An angry Montague was a scary thing to behold.

In my momentary distraction, several rounds punched into my glutes, launching me forward. I tucked into a roll and got to my feet.

"Shooting someone in the ass? Really?"

Three of the seventh ring's inhabitants must have thought I was done. The look of surprise on their faces as I unleashed Grim Whisper, firing three times, hitting all three of them in the chest, was priceless.

The skirmish was over before I knew it. I walked around and over the groaning and cursing unwelcoming committee. I thought the station was pungent before, but now we had achieved new heights of odor.

"Watching you fight nearly got me perforated. Daystrider saved my ass."

"You were supposed to be fighting, not watching," Monty said, gesturing.

"What style of fighting was that? *Krav magus*? It looked devastating."

"Every battle mage is taught close-quarters combat. With and without magic."

"Why not use the Sorrows?" I asked. "Would've been faster."

"That would have been excessive for this group. We were trying to keep them alive, remember?" he said, turning his face away. "Although, those persuader rounds may kill them from dysentery."

"Hey, I managed to keep them all mostly intact. Broke a few, but they're all still breathing. I was tempted,"—I glanced at the last three I dropped—"*really* tempted with those three, though."

Monty stood, holding an extra pungent mage in a lattice. It

reminded me of the one Esti used on Peaches, and my rage threatened to break free. This scrawny mage looked like he was in his early twenties—it was hard to tell with mages, since they aged slowly.

He was dressed in dirty rags, and was barefoot. Parts of his hair were matted down with dirt and debris. Judging from the grime, which was basically everywhere, his skin hadn't been in the proximity of water in years.

"Let me go," the mage said. "I'm nobody. I can't hurt you. I don't know anything."

"What's your name?" Monty asked. "Why did you attack us?"

"Berm, my name is Berm. I'm Berm," he answered nervously, looking around. "The Director,"—Berm continued, his eyes darting between Monty and me, "she said to take out anyone who gets off at this station. There's a reward out for you two."

"A reward?" I asked. "How much?"

"A month...She promised whoever finished you, a month."

"A month? A month of what?"

"A month of rations," Berm answered, staring at me. "You're not from the Market, are you? I can tell. You're clean...too clean. Not from the seventh, no. You're from outside, right? Not from the Market."

"No, we aren't," I said, keeping my distance. "We need to find someone, and then we're out of here."

Berm laughed and then hissed himself quiet. "Out of here? The whole seventh ring is coming for you," he said with a giggle, looking around. "You're not leaving here—not alive, at least."

"We'll see about that," I said. "Monty, can you take care of him, hellhound style?"

Berm scrunched his eyes closed, turning to Monty. "If you're going to kill me, can you make it fast, please? I don't like pain."

"Indeed," Monty said and began to gesture. "This will only take a moment."

Monty finished gesturing and produced three enormous

Peaches-worthy sausages and handed them to me. I placed them on the lattice next to Berm.

"Take these and disappear," I said in a low voice. "If I see you attacking us again, I'm going to make sure you hurt."

Berm opened his eyes wide.

"You're not...you're not going to kill me?" he asked, managing to open them wider when he saw the sausages. Monty removed the lattice, and Berm snatched up the sausages, vanishing them into his coat.

"No, we're not going to kill you...today," I said. "Make sure we don't see you again."

"Thank you, thank you," Berm said, pointing at us. "You won't see me again, that's for sure. You need to go back, before *he* smells you. He likes the tunnels...If he smells you...you're done—lunch time. Get out now...now. Before it's too late."

Berm ran to the end of the station and down into the tracks, disappearing silently into the darkness.

"Starving mages in the seventh ring," I said, my voice laced with simmering rage. "Still don't think we need to do something about Tessa?"

"*We* can't," Monty said. "But I'm certain we can make sure that this situation is addressed, somehow."

"Good, starting with pounding Tessa, I hope."

"That will be unlikely," Monty answered, still looking in the direction Berm had disappeared in. "The Moving Market is a necessary evil and provides goods unavailable elsewhere. Too many powerful individuals profit from it."

"So, she's just going to get a stern talking to? A slap on the wrist?"

"It will be dealt with," Monty said, his voice filled with enough menace to make me pause. "You have my word."

"Just make sure I'm there when it happens."

"Done. Let's locate Roque—if Tessa promised a month's worth of rations, we are in serious danger."

"We can't roam the seventh ring with a bounty on our heads," I said. "They will swarm us, and I don't have that many persuader rounds."

Monty headed into a tunnel and then stopped suddenly, causing me to nearly knock him down.

"Now may be a good time to switch to entropy rounds," Monty said under his breath. "It seems our search will be short."

"What? Why?" I asked, looking around in the darkness. "What's going on?"

"Do it slowly and without any sudden movements."

"Why didn't you kill him?" a voice asked from the darkness.

The throaty words floated over to us in the tunnel. Whoever or whatever was speaking was just this side of ginormous. I let my senses expand and felt a familiar presence, which encouraged me to subtly switch out my magazines. If I was right, and I really hoped I wasn't, things had just gotten a whole lot worse.

"Monty?" I asked, quietly switching the magazines to entropy rounds. "When Roque took the drake's blood, you mentioned a mutation."

"Yes, it completely undid his body, without diminishing his ability to cast."

"What *exactly* did he mutate into?"

"That is actually a fascinating question," Monty said, keeping his voice even. "It seems the runic energy in the blood completely reconstructed his body, giving it a new shape."

"A new shape?"

A low rumble filled the tunnel behind us, and I sensed the motion. Monty and I both turned to look into the face of the one creature that was truly fear-inducing.

A dragon.

The dim light from the tunnel was completely obscured, and I realized it was due to the dragon's body blocking most of the available light. Monty released an orb of light, illuminating an enormous body that took up almost all of the tunnel. Another low rumble filled the tunnel as it moved toward us, gouging the stone with its claws. Huge gashes appeared in the tunnel floor as it approached.

It crawled over to where we stood, and loomed, looking down. Turning its head slightly, it focused on Monty. Yellow eyes glimmered with violet energy as it leaned in closer. Dragons—up close—were truly, unmistakably petrifying.

"*That* new shape," Monty said. "Hello, Roque."

TWENTY-NINE

"Why didn't you kill the mage, Montague?" Roque asked. "He attacked you and deserved to die."

"He was no threat."

"Are you saying he was innocent?" Roque roared. "He attacked you!"

Monty remained calm and stared up at Roque's eyes. My first inclination was to empty Grim Whisper into Roque's face and run down the tunnel. To that end my hand drifted near my holster, but Monty shook his head slightly.

"I didn't say he was innocent, I said he was no threat."

"He tried to kill you." Roque glanced at the groaning unwelcome committee. "They all did."

"True," Monty said, looking at the prone bodies of our attackers. "But they have been manipulated and forced to act against their best wishes."

"They are all corrupt," Roque replied, "and worthy of death."

"They are all hungry," Monty said, staring at Roque, "and worthy of care. If you attack them"—Monty's hands went bright violet with black overtones—"I will be forced to stop you."

"You would dare face me for these worthless scum of the

159

seventh ring?" Roque asked. "You would race to your death to protect these insignificant specks of dust?"

"That will depend on you," Monty said. "We can do this easy, or we can do this hard, but you will not be touching them. The choice is yours."

"Are you sure you want to anger the already angry dragon?" I muttered, rubbing my still sore butt cheek. "He seems to dislike everyone from the seventh ring, and they *did* try to kill us."

"That doesn't mean they need to die," Monty answered quietly, still looking at Roque. "What they need is to be free of Tessa's influence. This dragon will not be killing anyone in my presence."

In that moment, I didn't know who was scarier. Of course, Roque was a dragon, and I had almost joined the rest of the unwelcoming committee in losing bowel control just from standing in front of him. Monty, on the other hand, was unleashing his best Gandalf 'you shall not blast' vibe at Roque. It was a standoff of epic proportions.

It was time for diplomacy.

I stepped in front of Monty and stared down Roque.

"I'm guessing you control the seventh ring, right?" I asked. "I mean, unless there's another dragon out here, you're the boss, no matter what Tessa says."

"The seventh ring is mine!" Roque roared again. "It is my dominion!"

"Right, exactly," I said, nodding. "You're this powerful dragon, correct?"

"Would you like me to demonstrate my power—on you?"

"Not really, thanks," I answered quickly. "But I do have a question. If this is your dominion, why do you let Tessa control the population?"

"She controls nothing!" Roque answered. "They cower before me in fear. I rule this ring, not Tessa."

"Those guys"—I pointed to the committee— "are starving, and she controls them. Are you saying she controls you, too?"

"No one controls me!" Roque roared loud enough to make the tunnel shake.

"Are you trying to get him angrier?" Monty asked, pulling me back a few steps. "This tunnel is unstable as it is."

"I got this," I said. "He's right where I want him."

"Where's that? Crushing us with a collapsed tunnel?"

I held up a hand, stilled my trembling legs and stepped closer to Roque. This was either going to work or I was going to be flattened dragon dinner.

"You think you rule this ring, but you don't. For all your power, you are a figurehead—worse, you're a deterrent. Tessa keeps you around to keep the population under control. Between letting you roam free and starving the ring, she can have them do whatever she wants—like coming after us. Face it, you're nothing but Tessa's pet monster."

Roque let out another massive roar. This time it looked like he was going to bring down the tunnel around us. Chunks of the ceiling started crashing into the floor of the tunnel.

Monty ran over to the committee, gestured and cast a large dome of golden energy over them. Large pieces of stone hit the sphere and bounced off, adding the crashing of stone to the roars of a dragon. I ran back into the sphere.

"I'd say that could have gone better," Monty said, as we stood in the center of the sphere. "Do you have any other ideas?"

"I do, but this one is risky."

"Riskier than an enraged dragon crushing us to death?"

"I'm going to siphon some of his energy and calm him down."

"Simon, no!" Monty yelled. "You can't do that. This isn't Slif. Roque is a full dragon mage. You siphon too much of his power, you *will* die."

"I'm open to suggestions!" I yelled back. "Can *you* calm him down before we're buried alive?"

I knew the answer before he said a word. I saw the sweat forming on his brow. He might have healed himself, but he was still recovering from our fight with Esti. If I didn't do something, the sphere would collapse and we would all be crushed.

"And maintain this shield?" he answered with some strain as another large chunk of stone bounced off the sphere. "No. No, I can't do both."

Sometimes the angry, irrational response doesn't come because of a lie. Many times, it comes because we've been confronted by a truth we don't want to face. On some level, Roque knew I was right; it didn't make it any easier to accept, but it was the truth. Tessa was using Roque like a guard dog for the seventh ring—well, in this case, a guard dragon.

I stepped outside of the sphere. The crashing of stone, along with the roars, made for a deafening combination. I figured Roque was going to be our supply of dragon's blood. Somehow, asking him didn't seem like a viable plan at the moment. It's not like I could say: *Hey, Roque, how about a pint? You know, for the road? Then we'll leave you alone to feed on the inhabitants of the seventh ring.*

I drew Ebonsoul and stepped close to Roque's body. He was still in full tantrum mode and would collapse the tunnel in on us any second. I took a moment to look back at Monty, who shook his head.

This was going to hurt on an epic scale. I found a gap between the scales on Roque's body, took a deep breath, and plunged my blade into the dragon.

"Time to embrace the suck," I said as the siphon started flooding my body with energy. "Oh...fuck."

The tunnel exploded with violet energy as the rest of the ceiling collapsed.

THIRTY

"Is he dead?" a voice said.

"He should be," Monty said. "But he has surprised me in the past."

"How did he survive that siphon? It should have blasted him to dust."

"He's too dense to die," Monty said. "You can open your eyes now, Simon. I know you're conscious."

"Are you sure I'm not dead?" I asked. "I feel dead, or at least mostly dead."

"Mostly dead means slightly alive," Monty replied. "Which is the natural state of your brain cells."

Monty jabbed a finger into my side—hard.

"Are you sure you two are friends?" the voice asked. "You realize he just siphoned me *out* of my dragon form? By all accounts, he should be a blasted pile of dust."

"I am aware," Monty answered, curtly. "I also know he survived the process."

Monty poked my side again—harder.

"Ow," I said, reflexively moving to the side and getting

unsteadily to my feet. "Fine, I'm not dead. But it feels like a truck landed on me—several of them, in fact."

"I managed to extend the sphere at the last second," Monty answered, "with a little help. You were mostly unscathed, at least externally."

"Right now, I'm feeling entirely quanked."

"Do you even know what that means?"

"Overpowered by fatigue, and what you get when you place armor on a duck."

"The former is impressive, while the latter is just gibberish," Monty said. "If you're done lounging, we have things to do."

"For the record, I wasn't lounging. I was contemplating some of my life choices. Like working with a volatile mage."

"Introspection is a worthy endeavor—perhaps one best shared with a favorite *bondmate*?"

"You're right," I said soberly. "We have things to do."

"Indeed," Monty answered with a nod.

Monty's words had energized me. We couldn't lose sight of what we were doing: rescuing Peaches, pounding Esti, finding Chi, and getting out of Japan before Fumiko caught up to us.

"Who's that?" I asked, motioning with my chin at the tall, clean-shaven, Liam Neeson look-alike standing next to Monty. He was dressed in a mageform suit that coruscated from the light of Monty's orb. When I looked closer, I saw that they were scales: actual miniature scales. "Wait, is that you, Rocky?"

Monty winced at my pronunciation.

Roque gave me a tight smile. "Close enough."

I looked at Monty. "He pulled a Slif?" I asked. "Talk about wearing dragonscale. That's really next level."

"Actually, all dragons can morph their forms from human to dragon," Monty said, using his wikimage voice. "Roque was trapped in his dragon form."

"Let me guess. Tessa?"

Roque nodded. "She had placed a temporal trap on my dragon

form, locking it in place. When you siphoned my life force, the trap didn't have enough energy to keep me in dragon form. The structural runic integrity of the stasis collapsed, freeing me."

"So *magespeak* is a real thing—got it," I said. "It wouldn't have been easier to say, 'The siphon freed me by sucking out my energy like a vacuum'?"

"Probably," Roque said, moving around the rubble. "I still don't know how you survived. You should be dead several times over."

I glanced at Monty, who gave me the 'we don't need to go into that detail' look.

"I'm wearing Daystrider armor," I said quickly, "and I've been practicing my runic defense. I'm sure a combination of the two combined to construct a lattice of nullification energy that funneled the siphoned energy into an ethereal repository to be drawn upon at a later date. Or something like that."

Roque looked at Monty, who just stared at me.

"I have to say," Roque started, "that happens to be the most extensive bullshit answer I've ever heard. Is that how mages sound to you?"

"Pretty much all the time, yes," I said, glancing at Monty. "At least when I can understand the language being spoken."

Monty almost smiled and looked away.

"We'd prefer not to say how he survived the collapse and the siphon," Monty said after a few seconds. "It's something Simon would rather not share."

Roque nodded and looked at me. "Wouldn't it have been easier to say, 'I'd rather not say'?"

"Point taken," I said. "I don't mean to offend, but Monty mentioned something about you being out of your mind?"

"I was, initially. It was one of the reasons I ended up here. In one of my more lucid moments, I was searching for a way to control the effects of the drake's blood."

"That kind of makes sense. If any place was going to have a

way to help you, it would be the Moving Market."

"The rage and resentment I held for the Golden Circle, for my erasure, drove me to do things I'm not proud of," Roque said, looking at Monty. "Your father and uncle saved me, even if I didn't see it at the time."

"The erasure saved you?" I asked, confused. "How would stripping your powers save you?"

"I had gone dark, way past dark, and had gotten a taste for killing," Roque answered, his voice grim. "After the erasure, when I drank the drake's blood, I was planning to go back and lay waste to the Golden Circle and everyone in it, starting with Connor and Dex."

"Drake's blood? I thought you drank dragon's blood?"

"No, they stopped me before I could get that far. I did the next best—or worst thing."

"What did you do that's worse than drinking drake's blood?"

"I cast Alder's Permutation on myself."

"Holy sh—"

"Yes. I was mad with regret, rage, and a desire for vengeance," Roque said, looking away as if reliving the moment in his memory. "They could have easily torn me to pieces. Have you met them? I don't know what I was thinking."

"I'm familiar with them, yes," I said, looking at Monty.

"Even in my drake form, I was no match for their combined power," Roque continued. "So, I did what I thought necessary. I crossed over into full dragon."

"Crossed over?"

"There is a variation to the permutation that allows for a radical transformation. Using the drake blood, I accelerated the process and transformed into a full dragon."

"That sounds like suicide," I said. "Doesn't Alder's kill the target once it's run its course?"

"What did I care about my life? I wanted vengeance, and they stood in my way. Even after all that, Connor and Dex saved me."

"What did they do?" I asked, curious as to how two mages could stand against a full dragon. "What did they use?"

"Connor was nearly an Archmage and Dexter is a temporal master. Together they isolated the permutation, but by then it was too late. The damage had been done. My mind had been seared by the casting."

"Yet they didn't kill you," I said. "They must have thought there was a solution. A way to reverse it."

"Connor did," Roque said. "Dex thought it was best to keep me forcibly restrained. Connor disagreed. They argued, along with the Golden Circle elders. It became violent. Some of the elders wanted to use me as a weapon. Both Connor and Dex opposed them. Things escalated, and in the chaos that followed, I escaped. Turns out Dex was right—it wasn't too long before I started having the seizures."

"Seizures? From the permutation?"

"He started transforming," Monty said. "Attacking mages while in dragon form."

"The seizures didn't last long at first; but, each time I had an episode, they lasted a little longer, until I was in dragon form most of the time. That's when I came here."

"Why here of all places?" I asked. "The seventh ring doesn't exactly scream 'safe dragon habitat.'"

"All of the sects were looking for me," Roque said. "The Dark Council wanted me captured or dead. I needed to get away. Someone told me they had a way to stop the seizures in the Moving Market. It was my last chance."

"Judging from your earlier performance, someone lied to you."

"When I discovered the treatment was a lie, I fled to the outer rings. No one dared to follow, and everyone left me alone. It wasn't too long after that I met Tessa."

"Well, shit," I said. "Hearing all that is going to make this request even harder."

"Request? What do you need?"

"We're here for blood," I said. "Specifically—dragon's blood."

THIRTY-ONE

"Are you insane?" Roque asked, raising his voice. "Did you not hear one word I just said!"

The last thing I wanted was an agitated dragon. Somehow, I didn't think mentioning how low the sun was getting was going to help in this case.

"Of course we heard you, but this isn't just about you," I said, turning to Monty. "Monty, is there a chance Dex can help him?"

Monty narrowed his eyes at Roque.

"In his current state, the permutation is dormant," Monty said. "I don't know how you did it, or how long it will last, but Uncle Dex can at the very least increase the duration of the suppression, if you go to him."

"Dex wanted to contain me," Roque said. "What about Connor? Where is he?'

Monty looked away as his features darkened. It was a moment that made me realize we all deal with loss in our own way; he may not have been overly close to Connor, but he was still his father.

"Connor...Connor passed away," I said when Monty didn't

answer. "There was a situation at the Golden Circle. Some mages wanted to take over, and Monty's dad managed to stop them."

"I'm sorry for your loss," Roque said. "Connor was a good man and a gifted mage."

"Thank you," Monty said when he had gathered himself. "The blood is urgent to our current mission."

"You don't know what you're asking," Roque said, shaking his head. "A small dose will drive you insane; a large dose—will kill you. Even if you survived the siphon, you won't survive this."

"I don't have a choice."

I took a deep breath, explained the situation to Roque and told him everything.

"Bloody hell," he said under his breath. "You're immortal?"

"More like cursed alive, but yes."

"And bonded to a hellhound and to this vampire Michiko you need to find?"

"Yes," I said. "If I don't act fast, they'll starve him and unleash him on Japan."

"What about the vampire? You're going to save a vampire?"

"Yes. If they kill her—I don't know what happens to me and this blade, but I can tell you what will happen to the Dark Council in New York."

"War," Monty said. "It will be the start of a second Supernatural War."

"Who *are* you?" Roque asked, looking at me in disbelief. "I thought my life was difficult."

"It's complicated," I said, setting my jaw and staring into Roque's eyes. "I'd rather you gave me the blood willingly. Would it help if I said please?"

"Let me see your blade," Roque said, extending a hand. "Two drops will imbue you with power to rival any low-level mage."

"What happens after two drops?"

"Three drops can magnify those powers considerably—and

put you close to an Archmage in ability," Roque said. "But, there are conditions."

"Aren't there always?" I asked. "This is the part where you say I implode in a spectacular fashion or agonizingly disintegrate into a pile of molten ash."

"Close," Roque said. "Two or three drops will give you access to phenomenal power. The power is temporary...but the effects can be permanent."

"Temporary? Do you know how long it will last?"

"That will depend on you and your capacity to deal with the blood," Roque answered. "I don't know anyone who has taken three drops and survived, and most of those who took two became insane—right before suffering a fatal cardiac event."

"What happened to those who took one drop?"

"It's an interesting process," Roque answered. "Apparently, one drop isn't enough to catalyze a runic energy change in the subject. With one drop, the blood is rapidly poisoned, resulting in a catastrophic failure of all major biological functions. Essentially, your poisoned blood shuts down every organ it infuses, resulting in—"

"Death," I finished. "I'm sensing a trend."

"I know you are different, and claim to be immortal, but my blood can kill you," Roque said. "I think this is a bad idea."

"Right now, it's the only idea. Two drops, please."

THIRTY-TWO

"Your blade is adequate, but there's one more complication," Roque said. "You'll need a special receptacle to contain the drops and cast a purification ritual. Tristan?"

"That is going to be more than a complication," Monty said. "I only know one person who may possess that kind of receptacle on short notice."

"Who? Aria?" I asked, sheathing Ebonsoul. "Tessa? Why do I need a receptacle?"

"Dragon blood can be absorbed through the skin," Monty said. "Without a proper receptacle, you can accidentally get too much."

"That sounds like a bad thing."

"The blood needs to be treated without removing its potency. You're not a dragon. Your body will attempt to reject it without the ritual."

"And the ritual?" Roque asked. "Can you do it?"

"I know it," Monty answered. "It's complicated, but not overly taxing."

"Just to be clear," Roque said, "the receptacle needs to be a runic nullifier that will not alter the integrity of the blood."

"Aria wouldn't possess something like that, and Tessa..." Monty started.

"Tessa tried to blow us up," I said. "She wouldn't give it to us, even if we asked."

"Correct," Monty said. "The only place we can locate something like that, within the timeframe we need, is Fordey Boutique."

"Oh, shit," I said. "She would never set foot in here—unless she were laying waste to the Market, ring by ring."

"Who are you referring to?" Roque asked. "She sounds incredibly dangerous."

"I'd rather face you, in your dragon form, than an angry TK," I said with a shudder. "If Monty asks her to come *here*, it won't be pretty. Are you sure that's the only option?"

"I'm certain," Monty said. "We need to get back to Japan— now. There's only one problem."

"What? Is Tessa shutting down the casting?"

"No," Monty said. "I may have overextended myself by casting the protection sphere."

"You broke your magic?" I asked, cocking my head to one side. "Eat one of your mage power bars. You know, the ones with new and improved, extra-dirt flavor—with a hint of moldy grass."

"Droll, as usual. My injuries have proven to be more extensive than I initially thought," Monty said. "The fact that the Market is in constant flux between spacetimes adds another layer of complication. I don't currently possess the necessary energy to effect a precise circle from inside the Moving Market."

"Basically what you're saying is...you broke your magic."

"Mages don't *break* their magic," Monty snapped. "It's just not possible."

"Sounds like yours is temporarily out of order. That sounds broken."

"I can cast," Roque said, interrupting us. "I've been to Japan. If you give me the exact coordinates, I can create a circle to where we need to go."

"If that's the case," I said, having a brilliant idea, "why not have Roque create a circle directly to Fordey?"

"No, for the simple reason that I enjoy the process of breathing," Monty answered with a glare. "If we teleport a dragon into Fordey Boutique, what do *you* think the outcome will be?"

"A dragon, detective, and mage puree served by one Chef TK. Sorry, bad idea."

"This TK sounds dangerous," Roque said. "Are you sure we want to meet her?"

"Want is a strong word," I said. "We *need* to meet her for the dragon's blood collector thingamabob, but I wouldn't say we *want* to meet her, per se."

"It's not a thingamabob," Monty said as he started gesturing. "The receptacle is called a runic nullifier."

Monty traced runes in the air in front of Roque, who studied them intently.

"Are you sure you can do this?" I asked Roque. "I'd rather not end up in the Arctic, or in several parts."

"I'm confident I can handle a teleport out of the Moving Market," Roque answered. "I may not be on Dex's level, but I can hold my own."

"Holding your own doesn't inspire confidence," I said. "Are you sure you can't do this, Monty?"

"Tristan, are you certain of this location? It's rather remote."

"Her brother gave us two locations," Monty answered. "This one makes more sense from a defensive position to draw in an enemy."

"Are you sure about this, Monty? He's probably rusty in the teleportation circle department."

"Roque can handle it, unless you want to wait for Tessa. I'm sure she'll dispatch the Doorman to come search through the rubble."

"You know what? There's no time like the present to get out of Dodge."

THIRTY-THREE

Roque began the cast of a violet circle on the ground. I saw him wince and clench his jaw as he released the energy forming the circle.

"You okay?" I asked, worried. "Are you sure you can do this?"

"Of course," he said, nodding his head with a tight smile. "It's been some time since I cast. Runic use is much easier as a dragon."

"I bet," I said, looking at Monty as I stepped to the side while Roque worked. "You better FedEx his ass to Dex as soon as we get the blood. I think he's reverting back to tall, dark, and scaly."

"It's a complicated cast," Monty muttered under his breath. "He has to pinpoint the location, then factor in the Market's movements while creating a trajectory for us to arrive. It's like threading a needle on a trampoline during an earthquake."

"That really boosted my confidence in his ability to do this."

I looked over to where Roque was still tracing runes in the air. Violet symbols filled the circle below him as sweat formed on his brow.

"Almost there," he said with a grunt. "Then we can leave."

"I don't trust him," I muttered under my breath. "He seems to be barely keeping it together. If he goes full dragon in Japan, Fumiko won't bother with politeness. She'll blast us on sight."

"I will check the cast before he activates the circle," Monty assured me. "Once we get to Japan, I will contact both TK and my uncle."

"I'm telling you, Monty, I may not know energy manipulation like you do, but he seems off."

"We have very little choice at the moment," Monty said. "Unless you'd like to cast a teleportation circle that savagely dismantles our bodies in transit? Like I said, I'll check the circle before we go."

"How soon before your broken magic is fixed?"

"My magic—is not broken…merely taxed beyond my current capabilities at the moment. I should be near full strength by the time we reach Japan."

Something was off, but Monty wasn't sharing.

Just then, Roque nodded and lowered his arms. The violet circle pulsed with energy. Monty stepped over and began examining the symbols.

"Well done," Monty said with a nod of approval. "This is serviceable and should put us in the shrine."

"I'm glad you think so," Roque answered, slightly winded. "It's been a while. That was unexpectedly difficult."

Another explosion rocked the tunnel behind us. We all turned to look, but the dust and debris was too thick.

"It would seem Tessa has grown tired of waiting," Monty said, stepping into the circle. "Let's go."

"I think that's our signal to vacate the premises," I said. "You ready, Rocky?"

In the distance, I could just make out a figure running towards us.

The Doorman.

Red orbs raced around him as he got closer. His silver staff gave off a soft glow as he increased his pace.

"It won't close in time," Roque said, looking at the symbols, and then looking off into the direction of the Doorman. "The Doorman will get through."

"What are you talking about?"

"The circle—it won't close...It won't...Ahhh."

Roque squeezed his head as he staggered back a step. He looked at me, and I could see violet energy glimmer in his eyes. He slid forward in a blur, and drew Ebonsoul from its sheath.

"What the hell? What are you doing?"

"No time," Roque said. "We have to do this now!"

"What are you talking—?

Roque sliced across his hand in one fluid motion, reached across, gripping my wrist before I could react, and cut across my palm.

"I'm sorry, Simon," Roque said. "I hope this works."

"Fuck!" I said, looking at the wound in my hand. "Are you insane?"

In another moment, Roque resheathed Ebonsoul, clasped my hand and placed his wound over mine.

"What are you doing?" I said, the shock reaching me before the pain. "We need a receptacle!"

"I'm sorry it had to be this way," Roque said. "I won't be joining you today."

He shoved me back into the circle and gestured. Violet light erupted in my hand as intense pain shot up my arm, bringing me to my knees.

"No!" Monty tried to step out of the circle, but a wall of energy kept us inside. "Don't do this, Roque. Uncle Dex can help you."

"Go save your hellhound and the vampire, Simon," Roque said, his skin transforming to scales, as his body expanded.

"Thank you for believing in me, Tristan, but I think it's too late for help."

I saw Roque revert back to full dragon form as the Doorman closed on him. He looked back one last time, roared, and slammed his body into the ceiling, collapsing the tunnel as a violet flash blinded me.

THIRTY-FOUR

We arrived in Japan at night. I looked around, nearly losing my balance; I placed a hand on the ground to stabilize myself. We were in some kind of stone building, but I couldn't make out the details. I lay still on the floor until the room stopped spinning. The cool stone felt good against my face.

"Whaft did he dosh?" I said, slurring my words. "Monthee, I donth feels so goof."

My body flushed hotter than it ever had been, Monty was saying words faster than I had ever heard. All of my senses were firing, but nothing was making sense. More pain wracked my body, and I screamed.

When the agony subsided, I grabbed Monty by the sleeve and tugged until he looked at me.

"I can hear purple," I said, the slurring gone. "But red tastes horrible. Don't eat the red."

"Stop talking," Monty said. "You're delirious from the dragon's blood. Bloody hell, was he trying to kill you?"

I opened my hand and violet light shot upward. Monty grabbed my hand, forcing it closed—plunging us into darkness again.

"Purple is a pretty color," I said. "It smells so purple."

"I need you here—now," Monty said next to me. "Dragon's blood, yes. Not drake's blood. I don't know how many drops...a gashful! He sliced his hand and then sliced Simon. The wound isn't healing. Yes, he's still alive. Don't ask me how. Just get here, now!"

"Hey, Trissy...Trissy," I said. "You know what would fix this? Hellhound slobber. Do you have any?"

"I'm currently all out of slobber. Don't move. Help is coming."

"Hell is coming? So run, you cur...run! You tell them I'm coming and hell's coming with me!" I yelled. "When is hell coming, Wyatt?"

A part of my mind, coldly calculated that I was currently on my way to batshit town for permanent residency. Whatever the dragon's blood had done was slowly and finally, zillerfrying my remaining brain cells. This realization hit me gradually, packed its bags, and quietly exited my mind, taking the voice of reason with it.

"Simon, stop talking," Monty hissed at me. "Where the bloody hell is he?"

I hissed back and pointed at Monty.

"Don't you black mamba me, kiddo."

A green flash filled the room, and I saw a portal open. I sensed two people enter the building we were in.

"Sorry for the delay, boy." A man's voice. "I figured I'd get some help for this one."

"How is he?" A woman's voice. "The energy signature is significant."

"My energy level is over nine-thousand!" I said, turning to the voices.

"Sliding deeper into insanity as you can see," Monty said. "Not that he wasn't halfway on the slope to start with. Help him."

"That's what I'm here to do, Tristan. Now move back. Dex,

place a temporal pocket around him. Let's see if we can arrest the effect of the blood."

"Don't arrest me!" I yelled. "I shot the sheriff, but I didn't shoot no deputy."

"How long has he been in delirium?" the woman asked as a green glow wrapped itself around me. "Dex, adjust the field and see if you can track the tainted blood."

"Since we arrived," Monty said. "He was lucid until the cut and shortly after, then he slipped into the state you see now."

"Understood," she said. "Open the hand, Dex."

"Bloody hell," the man said. "It's going to kill him if we don't get it under control, curse or no curse."

Purple light filled the room again, and I saw the faces of an old man and a scary lady. My brain struggled with the faces. I knew them.

"Flex! Tiki! You're here. Thank you for coming! I think someone threw up a wrench in the bucket I'm going to kick— wait, no, that's not right."

More pain stomped on my chest, grabbed me by the neck and started to punch me repeatedly in the face. I screamed then. I felt flames burning my body and saw violet energy wrapping itself around me.

"I'm going to sedate him," Tiki said. "His body is fighting the runes."

"Ignis…ignisvitamins!"

"Tristan, get a shield ready, now," Tiki said. "I can't believe he remembers the magic missile command, of all things. Remind me again, who thought that was a good idea?"

"Ignition!" I yelled, but nothing happened. I felt the power building up in me and needed to get it out. "It burns…I'm burning."

"Dex, he needs to be bled of that power somehow."

"Aye, lass," Flex said. "I'm giving the siphon all I've got."

"He used the blade on Roque," Monty said. "Can we simulate it?"

"Roque? The dragon?" Flex asked. "How did you face him?'

"Irrelevant," Tiki said. "If we use his blade, it will create an energy feedback loop. I'm fairly certain that will kill him, although why he isn't dead by now eludes me."

"Where is the blade?" Flex asked, looking around. "It's not in the sheath."

"Ssshhh." I put a finger to my lips and pointed to my chest. "It's in here. Secret pocket."

"He internalized it," Monty said. "Dissolved it into mist and absorbed it into his body instantly."

"Too much power," I muttered. "It's too...much...power."

"There's no way to do an erasure," Flex said. "He's bleeding off too much energy."

"Ignis." The word was coming to me. "Iggy Pop?"

"Tristan, get the shield over him. Now."

I saw Monty wiggle his fingers at me. I wiggled mine back and saw my hands covered in violet energy. When I looked down, my entire body was covered in the same energy. A dome of golden light materialized around me.

"By the power of numbskull...I have the power!"

"Dex, reinforce the shield—I'll add the portal. His curse is fighting to regulate the dragon's blood, and failing. We may lose him."

"Tiki, tiki, tiki torch," I said, patting her on the back of her hand. "No one is fighting. We are all peaceful warriors here, Fuu, you Samurai Champloo sandwich you."

More pretty colors wrapped themselves around me. It was a rainbow of goodness.

"Tiki torch?" Tiki said, sounding upset. "I'm sedating him —now."

"Try not to kill him, lass."

"Is that what we're doing?" Tiki said. "The nullification field is in place."

"Ignis...*Ignisvitae*," I finally managed. "That's it!"

The room erupted in violet light. All around me, I saw orbs of violet materialize. Suddenly, I heard a sound like raindrops, if raindrops were made of concrete.

"Shutting him down...now."

Those were the last words I heard before slipping into darkness.

THIRTY-FIVE

"**Y**ou should be dead—permanently."

It was TK.

She was wearing her usual black on black ensemble, except this outfit came complete with a deep hood, which she currently had over her head, providing an extra dose of menace.

I tried to sit up and found myself immobile. Green tendrils of energy wrapped themselves around my arms and legs, and buried themselves into the stone beneath me.

My everything ached, hurt and screamed at me with every breath I took. Even my hair was in agony.

"What the hell," I said with a groan. "Why does it feel like someone hit me with a wrecking ball...repeatedly?"

"How...are...you...alive?" TK asked. "The initial amount of dragon blood in your system should have destroyed you."

"I'm feeling pretty destroyed right now, trust me." I looked over at the restraints keeping me in place. "Are these things really necessary?"

"Yes."

I looked around. We were in a small, stone temple. The floor was covered with tatami mats, except where I lay. Shoji doors separated the space from the outside. From what I could tell, it was still night. I let my eyes adjust to the low-light conditions and looked around again. I noticed small, grapefruit-sized craters covering the ceiling and walls.

"Are those…"

"Yes."

"Did I…"

"Yes."

"You seem upset," I said, treading softly into this conversation. "What happened?"

"Before or after I had to encase the shrine in a nullification field?"

"After?" I asked, dreading the answer and hoping I didn't blast anyone.

If she had to enclose the entire shrine in a nullification field, things were nearly cataclysmic. It meant I was a threat to everything in the general area.

"You punched through Tristan's, Dexter's and my shields," TK answered. "Right before I was forced to disconnect you."

"Disconnect me?"

"Shut down your synapses."

"You turned off my brain?"

"It's more difficult than it sounds, especially when trying to keep the subject alive."

"I appreciate the 'keeping alive' part—thank you."

"We almost reconsidered that near the end—you were getting dangerous."

I didn't know what was scarier: the fact that she was able to discuss my demise with such ease, or that after I ingested dragon's blood and lost control, she thought I was *getting* dangerous.

My body felt like it had been beaten with a bag of hot hammers. The pain around my skull signaled that my brain was currently trying to crawl out of my head through my eyeballs.

"What time is it?" I asked with a groan. "How many hours have passed?"

"Early evening."

"Early evening?" I asked, confused. "It was early evening when we got here. We are still in Japan, right?"

She nodded. "We're in the vicinity," TK answered, looking outside. "You and Tristan arrived here last night."

"Last...night? I've been unconscious this whole time?"

"I wouldn't say unconscious; more like pre-conscious," TK said. "You were semi-responsive and managed to recall certain events, including, of course, the trigger for your magic missile. Other things eluded you, like how to get the energy coursing through you under control."

"I didn't quite manage that, did I?"

"You absorbed an obscene amount of dragon blood, which would've killed anyone else," TK started. "Then, you proceeded to unleash magic missiles—*after* I had sedated you."

"After you sedated me?"

"Did I stutter?"

"Not in the least," I said. "Please, continue."

"I had to shut down your entire synaptic system without disabling your autonomic system," TK said. "This allowed Dex to siphon and then shunt the energy away from us."

"Is that even possible?"

TK narrowed her eyes at me. "You're still here."

"True." I nodded slowly to avoid increasing the intensity of the drumline practicing in my skull. "Is Monty? Dex?"

"All of us are fine, if not somewhat worse for wear," TK said. "I understand the Blood Hunters absconded with your hellhound."

"I'm getting him back," I said, feeling a surge of energy I'd never felt before. "Esti and her psychohunters *will* regret taking him."

"Calm down before I add more restraints," TK said, adding more restraints.

"But you're already adding—"

"Because you haven't calmed down. Now, calm down and wait for the others."

I closed my eyes and took a deep breath, letting it out slowly.

"Why am I not dead?" I asked, looking up at the cratered ceiling. "That dragon's blood should've ended me."

"By all rights you should be deceased, boy," Dex said, walking into the room. "But we both know how well that takes with you."

"Hello, Dex," I said, genuinely happy to see him. "What did the—"

"Ach—one second, boy," Dex said, looking around the interior. He waved a hand and whispered some words, making all of the craters disappear. "You were saying?"

Dexter was dressed in a pair of dark green boxers covered by a dark gray robe with a repeated raven motif. His long hair was pulled back in a braid and finished off with a black hair clip shaped like a raven in mid-flight.

"Didn't have a chance to get dressed?" I asked, eyeing the attire. "Were you busy?"

"I was just getting started when my nephew called," Dex answered with a wink and looked down. "What do you mean, I'm not dressed? This robe was a gift from Mo."

I still didn't understand how anyone could be in a relationship with the Morrigan, but that spoke volumes about Dex. As a mage, he was insanely powerful. The fact that the Morrigan, someone even scarier than TK, took an interest in him still boggled my brain.

The resemblance with Monty always threw me. Where Monty was tall and thin, Dex was a little shorter and rounded out. His salt-and-pepper hair was long like Monty's, but the face gave it away. Dex was an older version of Monty with laugh lines —something I was sure Monty's face would never suffer from.

"How is the Golden Circle these days?" I said. "I'd get up, but TK feels this is safer."

"Because it is," TK said. "I'm not in the mood to calm him down again."

"Let him free," Dex said. "If he gets out of control, I'll put him down."

"That," TK said with a small smile as she waved a hand, undoing the restraints, "is something I'd like to see."

There was something seriously wrong with the both of them. I got unsteadily to my feet and moved over to a short bench that sat along the wall. Dex sat down next to me with a grunt.

"The Circle chafes, boy," Dex said. "I'm not meant for offices or 'meetings' and the like. I need to be out in the world. Roaming free."

"Like a wild animal," TK said.

"Aye," Dex answered. "Free with nothing and no one to hold me down."

"Except the Morrigan," TK replied. "Does she know about this 'freedom' of yours?"

"We have an understanding of sorts," Dex answered quickly. "I need my space and she doesn't care. It's all compromise."

I laughed and instantly regretted it. Pain did a Mexican hat dance across my skull and proceeded to sashay down the rest of my body, swinging a sledgehammer of agony.

"I think you'd make a good teacher," I said after catching my breath. "You may not like the Golden Circle, but maybe a substitute teacher?"

"Please, don't give him any ideas," TK said. "The last thing we need is Dex teaching the next generation of mages."

"Ach," Dex said, rubbing his chin Monty style. "It's an idea for another time. More importantly"—he slapped me in the back, reigniting all the pain—"how are you feeling?"

"Like an ogre's punching bag after being a chew toy for Peaches' dad."

"Aye," Dex said with a grunt. "We'd be concerned if it were otherwise."

I closed my eyes and laid my head back against the cool stone. Things couldn't get worse. Peaches was gone, Esti was out there with her psychohunters chasing after Chi, who was still missing, and I was wrecked.

I took a deep breath and let it out slowly.

A thrum of power vibrated through my body. It felt like I had hit the nerve in my elbow, setting off my funny bone. I never understood why it was called that; there was nothing funny about the sensation of being mildly electrocuted. I guess 'funny bone' was more acceptable than 'oh shit that hurts' bone.

"I can feel him," I said, opening my eyes in surprise. "I can feel Peaches."

THIRTY-SIX

Monty stepped quickly into the shrine.

"Is he relapsing?" Monty asked, looking around. "What happened? I just felt—"

"Whatever it is that you're doing," Dex said, his voice a warning as he glared, "you need to stop, boy."

I looked at the perplexed Monty.

"I know where Peaches is," I said. "I can feel him."

TK remained silent and stared as Dex shot to his feet.

"You can't go out there until we've determined the extent of the damage," Dex said, pointing to the shoji door. "It's too dangerous. Tell him, lass."

I let the power flow through me again.

"I know where he is, and I'm going to go get him."

"Wait," TK said, drawing all eyes to where she stood. "How do you feel?"

"Like I need to go get my hellhound."

"Understood," she said. "However, if you lose your mind in the middle of Japan, it will be a problem—a problem I helped create, and a problem I will have to fix. Answer my question."

I took a deep breath and did a mental inventory. I felt strong

—stronger than I had ever felt in my life, but that wasn't it. My bonds were clear, and for the first time I could feel each bond. I extended my hand and formed Ebonsoul instantly. The next second, I absorbed it without delay.

"I feel connected," I said, certain. "I feel whole."

TK nodded. "If you had said anything else, I'd be forced to restrain you again."

"And if I broke free?" I asked, feeling particularly suicidal in the moment.

"I'd reluctantly deliver your body to Haven...in pieces."

"Have I ever told you," I said, reining in my momentary lapse in self-preservation, "just how scary you are?"

"No need," TK answered, tracing green runes in the air. "I'm content being the bogeyman's bogeyman, if needs must."

"Are you daft, boy?" Dex said. "Just because you have some hair on your bollocks doesn't mean you wrestle the dragon."

His words reminded me of Roque.

"Simon," TK said, snapping my attention back to her. "Get your hellhound, secure the vampire, and teach the Blood Hunters a lesson."

"A lesson?"

"One that makes them reconsider ever touching those close to you," TK answered. "It needs to be swift, merciless, and brutal. You must leave no doubt in their minds that attacking you and yours was an error with fatal consequences. Give no quarter."

"Ach," Dex said, shaking his head. "You sound like the Badb."

"Who do you think taught me?" TK said with an arctic smile as a portal formed in front of her. "Remember what I said, Simon."

She stepped into the portal and disappeared.

"I didn't get to thank her," I said when the portal vanished. "Can you tell her I—?"

"I'll pass on the word," Dex said, looking around where the

portal was to make sure she was gone. "That is one fearsome woman."

"Scarier than the Morrigan?"

"My boy, nothing and no one is scarier than the dark goddess," Dex said with a smile. "She is insatiable in every way."

"You said dragon," I said, trying to deflect the conversation. "There's this dragon in the Moving Market. He's—"

"Roque," Monty said. "His permutation has been weakened and he needs help."

"Aye," Dex said. "You mentioned him earlier. You used the blade on him?"

"It severed a trap that had been keeping him in dragon form," Monty said.

"Tessa was keeping him locked as a dragon and using him as the seventh ring monster," I explained. "Can you help him?"

"Roque...I haven't heard that name in ages," Dex said. "I suppose I can pay the Market a visit. Looks like Tessa is overdue some Circle discipline."

"Tessa is a Golden Circle mage?" I asked. "Are you serious?"

"Was," Dex said. "But, she never had a head for the studies. Too driven by ambition and coin."

"She hasn't changed much. She's starving the seventh ring to control the population."

"I see," Dex said, his expression dark. "It may be time for new management at the Moving Market. Leave it to me."

"Your vampire is in Hokkaido," Monty said, looking at me. "We can use the shrine and locate her before Esti and the Blood Hunters find her."

"What are you talking about? They said five days...Esti said five days."

"Did you really think they were going to wait for you to deliver her to them?" Monty asked. "You believe Esti will act in good faith? She wants to kill you both."

"I thought...Fuck. You're right. How could I be so stupid?"

"Can't trust those Blood Hunters, boy. They see blood and get almost as bad as the creatures they hunt."

"How long will this last?"

"Blood hunters and vampires been fighting for centuries," Dex answered. "I don't see an end to that particular cog anytime soon."

"Not that," I said, outstretching my hands, letting the violet light escape from my palms. "This power—my abilities."

Dex shook his head. "No real way of telling. I've never encountered this situation before—immortals don't usually go around drinking dragon's blood. At least not without dying horrible deaths."

"That was helpful."

"I know," Dex said with a smile, putting his hand on my shoulder. "It's not my purview, but you can be certain of one thing, though."

"What?" I said, bracing myself for some pervy response. "You get more action than most mages half your age?"

"Hey! How did you know?" Dex said, clapping me on the back and nearly dislocating my shoulder in the process. He let out a throaty chuckle, then grew serious. "You can be certain of this"— he extended a finger at me—"they will be watching you now more than ever, Chosen of Kali."

He rubbed the finger by his nose, materialized a portal, and disappeared.

THIRTY-SEVEN

"What did TK mean when she said we're in the vicinity of Japan?" I asked. "Where are we?"

"This is the Mount Tokachi Refuge," Monty said. "We are currently in-between planes..."—He held up a hand.—"One moment."

Monty stopped gesturing, and a golden light flashed around the door for a second before fading. The cool night greeted us with silence. He opened the shoji door and stepped out of the small shrine right into the middle of nowhere.

"Where did you say we were?" I asked, looking around the area of the refuge. There was a small clearing, then a thick forest at its edge. From where I stood, it appeared like the trees were slowly advancing on the refuge.

"About a mile away from the Nakatomi residence—*Kuro Sakura no Shiro.*"

"Castle of the Black Cherry Blossoms—Black Blossom. That's not ominous at all."

"I don't believe the naming conventions for castles focus on the lighthearted and fun," Monty said. "I'm sure, in this case, it

197

has more to do with the indigenous trees in the are, than menace."

"They could still make it less dark."

"It is a little dark," Monty replied. "The castle is on the edge of the Tokachi plain, not far from Mount Tokachi. This forest begins here and extends past Black Blossom. The rumors are that it's more dangerous than *Aokigahara*."

"*Aokigahara*—the suicide forest? The one near Mount Fuji?"

"Yes, except I suspect this forest was dangerous for reasons connected to the Nakatomi household."

"Makes sense," I said, looking into the dense forest. "You have people disappearing into a forest at night, and you just happen to feed on people. It must have been like having your meals delivered to your doorstep."

"The fascinating part is that the forest near Mount Tokachi is virtually unknown, even to this day."

"Fascinating?" I said, looking into the night. "More like suppressed and creepy as hell. They probably kept it hidden to keep feeding."

"Try and pinpoint the location of your creature," Monty said, closing his eyes for a few seconds. "Black Blossom castle is"—he pointed north—"located in that direction. Over there."

"What is it with the castles?" I asked. "Why can't they be in the Duplex of Cozy Dumplings in the middle of Tokyo or something like that?"

"The Nakatomi family is ancient in the history of Japan, dating back to the pre-feudal era. Having a castle is only a small expression of their influence. Being in a remote location also ensured privacy, which I imagine was essential when you're a family of vampires."

Off in the distance, I could just make out the silhouette of a large structure I guessed was Black Blossom Castle. I sensed the subtle energy around the castle, but it didn't feel like Chi. I took a deep breath and focused on my bond with Peaches. His energy signature was slowly moving closer to our position.

"Good point. Are there any roads that lead to Black Blossom Castle?"

"None to my knowledge, and we will have to travel at night."

"They're coming, but moving slowly. At this rate, they'll get here by morning."

"Can you tell what direction?"

"I can feel Peaches that way" I said, pointing south. "It's distant, but he's moving toward us, not away."

"They must be transporting him," Monty said. "It's risky for them to be mobilizing at night, considering where they're going."

"Do you think there will be other vampires besides Chi?" I asked. "The last thing I want to do is fight ancient vampires *and* deal with Esti."

"It's possible, but unlikely. I think we'll only have to worry about Esti and her hunters," Monty replied, "not to mention, the Kuro Hyogikai."

"Fumiko will be after you for sure," I said. "You totally blew up that courtyard."

"If I recall, *you* blew up the courtyard."

"Your triggers—your explosion," I said. "She'll never believe *I* was the cause of that destruction. If we move now, we can avoid Fumiko and Esti until Black Blossom."

"Esti and her Blood Hunters will be out in force at daybreak."

"Do we know her numbers?"

"No, which needs to inform our strategy in dealing with them."

"We saw how effective a frontal attack was last time," I said. "The sorceresses are a game changer."

"Their influence can't be denied, which means we need to neutralize the runic component of the attack."

"They also wouldn't dare approach Chi at night when her

power is at its strongest," I said. "If I were hunting a vampire, I would wait until morning as well."

"Can you communicate with your creature?"

I closed my eyes and focused again, and got the equivalent of white noise.

"No. Whatever they're using to control him must be interrupting our communications. I can try harder."

"Logic would dictate that they will travel with him to lure you to a place of their choosing and eliminate you there."

"But they're headed to Black Blossom."

"It appears that way, yes," Monty said. "The wisest course of action would be to hinder you first. You pose a serious threat... and they want the blade."

"Ebonsoul would make getting rid of Chi easier, but not guaranteed. She's not exactly a soft target."

"They have sorceresses with them," Monty said, his voice low. "They can use blood magic to destroy your vampire at the source of her family's power."

"That would mean they would try to take Chi where she thinks she's the strongest?"

"I'm sure they're counting on her overconfidence. Esti will use the element of surprise and attack during the night. Your vampire will retaliate and walk into a trap."

"We have to get there first," I said. "If Esti launches an attack, Chi will think she's only facing the Blood Hunters."

"Much like we did," Monty replied, gesturing. "Your vampire will be unprepared for their response."

Chi was no pushover, but neither were we. The Blood Hunters had blindsided us with sorcery; it had cost us Peaches, and had nearly cost us our lives. If I was Esti, I would dangle Peaches to get my attention.

"Shit," I said. "This is bad. We need to get Peaches first."

"No," Monty said. "You're thinking emotionally, not rationally. We need to see if they are bringing him all the way to

Mount Tokachi. Remember, she knows you share a bond with him. If I were her, I'd use your hellhound—"

"To lure me away so I couldn't protect Chi. If I were Esti, I would dangle Peaches to get my attention and send another group to Black Blossom."

"That would be the prudent strategy: divide and conquer."

"She's expecting me to go after him first," I said. "She's counting on that."

"Like she said, it's your vulnerability. We can't underestimate her again."

As much as I hated to admit it, Monty was right. We needed to stop them at Black Blossom, and then get Peaches back.

THIRTY-EIGHT

"How do you feel?" Monty asked as we stepped into the forest. "Are you feeling lucid, in control?"

I let my senses expand and felt the undercurrent of energy. All around me, I felt threads of energy criss-crossing and joining. Everything was truly connected, I felt, as the dragon's blood coursed through my body. I could see myself getting used to this, if this was what mages felt on a regular basis. It was almost as good as javambrosia.

I was just about to answer when I heard the first arrow whisper quietly in the air. I pulled Monty out of the way as it buried itself into a nearby tree, missing him. A second longer and it would've hit Monty square in the back.

Several seconds later, more arrows flew at us. We moved behind trees and avoided becoming pincushions.

"Two teams?" Monty asked. "Or more?"

I nodded, feeling out the forest. "More—one team with Peaches a few miles back."

"Bait," Monty said, shaking out his hands. "What else?"

"Large group in the forest, spread out at intervals."

"They will act as obstacles, trying to slow us down." Monty

began tracing runes in the air. Dark violet symbols laced with red formed orbs and sped off. "Let's see if we can keep them busy."

"Another team in the castle," I said. "Shit, we're too late."

"Not yet, we aren't," Monty said. "How fast do you think you can move in your current state?"

"Probably blazing fast, why?"

"When you hear the signal, we head to the castle," Monty said, casting a series of golden runes on his body. "Ready?"

"Not really? What signal?"

More arrows whispered by, followed a few seconds later by screams.

"That signal. Run!"

He shifted to the side and then winked out of sight, Peaches-style. I unleashed some of my power and followed. Monty moved faster than I could see—I locked on to his energy signature and tried to keep up. We ran through the forest to a chorus of screams. As fast as we were moving, Blood Hunters still tried to hit us with arrows...and each time they tried, an orb of agony located them.

Ten minutes later, we were standing in front of the open gate at Black Blossom Castle. Monty reached back and drew the Sorrows. Screams still filled the night as Monty's rune-seeking orbs found the Blood Hunters.

"What were those things?" I asked, looking behind us. "I've never seen you use tracking orbs like that."

"Runic trackers," Monty said, a little short of breath. "They are keyed to the arrows, not the hunters."

"That explains the screams after they tried to perforate us."

"The trackers are dormant until they release an arrow, and then they follow the runic trail back to the hunter who fired the it. At least in the first phase."

"Do I want to know what happens in the second phase?"

"They start tracking the energy signature of the hunters."

"Devious and devastating," I said. "They don't know what's coming until it's too late."

"After our last run in, I realized we needed to use their strengths against them," Monty answered, moving forward. "Daystrider armor should keep us from falling prey to the blood arrows or LIT rounds, which I doubt they'll use."

"Which means blades," I said, materializing Ebonsoul. "Are we still using diplomacy?"

"I don't know what will happen to you if you kill a Blood Hunter," Monty said, narrowing his eyes and looking at me. "Your body is at its capacity. If you siphon more energy, it may tip you over the edge into another episode of last night."

"Right, no one needs that," I said, reabsorbing Ebonsoul. "No killing, but intense breakage works."

"Can you sense your vampire?"

I looked up and let my senses expand again. Chi's energy signature was somewhere near the top of the castle.

"Top floor," I said, looking at the top of the castle. "But I'm getting a serious energy signature lower in the middle of the building."

"What you're sensing is a cast of undoing," Monty said. "It's darker than blood magic."

"Is it too much to expect them to give up peacefully?"

Monty stared at me. "Yes," he said, his voice grim. "Esti is deranged in her quest for vengeance. She will never give up—peacefully or otherwise. Focus on the casting."

"We need to stop them first," I said as more screams filled the night. "What are the orbs tracking now? We left the forest."

"Seems like the second phase has begun," Monty said, looking behind us into the dense woods. "The trackers are now locking onto the hunters themselves. Any of them who are still standing…won't be for long."

"Did you?"

"Of course not," Monty said. "The only one we *may* need to end is Esti. There is no reasoning with that kind of madness."

I searched the forest with my heightened senses and breathed out a small sigh of relief. The hunters were in excruciating agony, but alive.

"Well, at least this forest doesn't have to go unnamed any more."

"You've decided to name it?"

"Yes," I said, listening to the screams and sobs filling the night. "The Wailing Forest sounds appropriate."

THIRTY-NINE

We crossed the outer gate and stepped to the front door. It was a massive, wooden affair, covered in angry black runes that pulsed with energy.

"How old do you think Black Blossom is?"

"Old enough to make us reconsider its destruction. This castle fortress must date back at least to the early 1600's, if not earlier."

"Meaning Fumiko will be royally pissed if we broke it?"

"To put it lightly," Monty said, looking at the wooden and stone structure. "She seemed very possessive of her country."

The area near the entrance was an ornate receiving area. A large stone wall encircled the property, ending at the outer gate, which resembled a series of Shinto shrine gates in sequence. The first gate at the wall was done in stone, whereas the following ten were made of wood and painted bright orange. I turned back to face the front door.

"That doesn't look like 'welcome home.'"

"Can you read it?" Monty asked. "Do you know what it says?"

I narrowed my eyes and discovered my newfound ability didn't automatically make it possible for me to read ancient Japanese, much less ancient runes.

"No," I said, shaking my head. "But I can tell you what the energy feels like."

"And that is?" Monty asked, stepping back from the door to view the entire surface. "I can't read these proto-runes."

"Basically, all I'm getting is a variation of: 'Dare to open this door, and meet your demise.' It's either that, or 'Don't be an idiot, run now while you still can.'"

Monty stared at me. "Are you sure you aren't relapsing?"

"I'm good," I said, pointing at the massive door. "You plan on deciphering these runes?"

"No, they are beyond me," Monty said. "I plan on letting you use the key."

"The key?" I asked, patting my pockets. "What key? I don't have the key."

"You do," Monty said. "Aim your hand at the door and trigger your magic missile."

"You just said Fumiko would be pissed if we broke this place."

"Which is why you're opening the door."

"What if it doesn't work?"

"Focus your energy at the door," Monty said, moving farther away and casting a shield. "Remember to focus."

I pointed my hand at the door, took a deep breath and focused my energy.

"Are you sure?"

"Absolutely. Don't forget to cover your face."

"With my shield?"

"If you think it can withstand the energy."

Now he had me concerned.

"How much power do you think I plan on unleashing?" I asked. "This is only a magic missile."

He waved me on to continue. "You can do this. Try not to obliterate the castle."

I took a deep breath and focused on the door, allowing the energy inside to accumulate.

"*Ignisvitae*," I said and pushed forward with my hand. For a second, nothing happened. I glanced at Monty. "I don't think it's going to—"

A blast of violet energy exploded from my hand, launching me back. I crashed into the stone wall opposite the entrance, with a bone-crushing thud.

"Ow," I said as I slid down the wall. My body blazed, dealing with the damage. By the time I reached the floor, I felt better. "That was unexpected."

Monty absorbed his shield and nodded. "Looks like you had the key after all."

I looked up and had a little trouble processing the image. The door, the frame, and the surrounding stone were missing. All that was left was a smooth, ten foot-wide gaping hole where there used to be a large wooden door.

"That was a magic missile?"

"Enhanced by dragon's blood, yes. Maybe switch out for persuaders, before you disintegrate everything and everyone?"

"Yeah...Yeah maybe that's a good idea," I said, switching magazines in favor of the persuaders. "Think I'll do that."

It took a few tries due to the shaking of my hands. Monty stepped up to the smoking hole, examining the edge of the blast.

"I'd say the dragon's blood has definitely increased the strength of your missile," he said, running a finger along the smooth stone. "It still needs some refining. With some practice, this could be truly devastating—if Fumiko and the Kuro Hyogikai don't crush you first."

I stared at him for a good five seconds.

"I hope you're enjoying yourself," I said. "You've turned me into a greater menace than you and Peaches combined."

"I strongly urge you not to use your magic missile inside the castle, unless absolutely necessary."

"Are you insane?" I said as we crossed the threshold into the castle proper. "I can't hit anyone with that thing. It will disintegrate them."

"Not necessarily," Monty said. "Against some beings, a blast like that would only be an attention-getter."

"I don't *want* to get their attention," I said, looking around the interior. "Can we not get their attention? Like ever?"

"Unlikely," Monty said. "As for attention, I'm sure that entrance has garnered some from the Blood Hunters."

I looked back at the gaping hole. "It wasn't exactly subtle, that's for sure."

"Stairs," Monty said, pointing one of the Sorrows. "We have to stop the casting."

FORTY

W e reached the next level and encountered a group of five women in a circle surrounded by black energy. The air was thick with power, and I had a hard time focusing on the women. The energy they were casting sent snake-like tendrils of black energy up into the ceiling.

"Casting?" I asked. "Those tendrils can't be good."

"They'll be used to restrain your vampire," Monty said. "Let's make sure they don't finish."

Each of the women was dressed in black robes with red accents along their edges, reminding me of renegade nuns—renegade nuns that controlled black runic energy designed to destroy an ancient vampire.

Two of the women noticed us and broke from the circle. I fired Grim Whisper, but my rounds vanished into a small portal that appeared in front of them.

"That may be problematic," I said, dodging to the side as black orbs of energy raced at me.

"Kill them," one of the remaining women from the circle said. "The ritual is almost complete. Don't let them interrupt us."

"Why is it always 'kill them'?" I asked, rolling to the side and firing again as more orbs tried to smash into me. More portals swallowed my rounds. "Why can't it be 'give them a stern warning' or 'stop them with a solid pounding'? Everything has to be so fatal."

"I'm sure they'll be open to conversation," Monty said, deflecting a black orb with his sword and unleashing several violet ones of his own, "right after you stop them with a solid pounding."

Monty closed the distance and engaged one of the sorceresses who broke the circle. He unleashed orbs, but they met the same defenses as my rounds, disappearing from sight. Both of the women drew swords.

"Simon...the ritual," Monty said, as both women attacked. "If it's completed, it will trap your vampire."

"I'm trying to shoot them, Monty," I said, firing again and missing. "The Sisters of the Black Hole keep swallowing my rounds."

"Use...your hands," he said, deflecting an orb and parrying a sword slash. "Just try not to obliterate them."

I holstered Grim Whisper and advanced on the circle, unleashing the power I held. Everything was accelerated. I blinkstepped forward, using the maneuver from the forest. I reappeared next to one of the renegade nuns, who greeted me with a black orb to the face. The impact spun me around, sending me into a wall.

I bounced off the wall as my body blazed. I focused the energy and made a fist. I concentrated on using less power, holding back the reservoir within.

"*Ignisvitae,*" I whispered, forming a large violet orb and releasing it into the air. I said the next word before I understood what I was saying. "*Captis.*"

The orb raced at the women and exploded into hundreds of smaller orbs, swarming and immobilizing all of the renegade nuns.

"You're too late," one of the women said, struggling against the restraint. "The ritual is complete. The vampire is ours."

Monty was staring at the renegade nuns and then back at me.

"How did you—?" he started.

"I don't know, but we need to help Chi."

"Upstairs—now." Monty gestured and several golden orbs launched from his hands, slamming into the nuns, knocking them unconscious. "Can't have them trying another ritual."

We ran for the stairs and headed up. Gunfire chewed up the top of the stairs as we reached the next floor, forcing us back down to take cover. Chi was entangled with the black tendrils as they wrapped around her limbs.

"Have you come to watch your vampire die?" Esti yelled, unloading another barrage of rounds at the stairs. "Right after she dies, we'll take care of your beast and get our blade back. Just be patient."

"I'm going to give you back your blade," I yelled back, "by burying it in your chest!"

FORTY-ONE

"Simon, leave this place," Chi said. "She has lost her mind. I'm beyond saving."

Chi's face was bruised, cut, and swollen. She hung in the air as the tendrils held her suspended. Her right arm was bent at an unnatural angle, while the fingers of her left hand were all twisted in different directions.

Esti laughed. "She has finally spoken a truth," Esti said, and spat on Chi. "You lying piece of scum. No one can save you now."

I ran up the stairs and rolled to the side, avoiding more gunfire, as Monty came up behind me, unleashing orbs and throwing up a shield.

Esti flicked her wrists and two long, runed blades materialized in her hands. I instantly recognized the runes as the same ones on the blood arrows. Getting stabbed by one of those would end badly—for me.

"You deal with Esti," Monty said. "I'll undo the tendrils."

Monty raced over to where Chi hung immobilized and began casting black runes that made me feel uneasy. I looked at Chi, and the rage inside me howled to be unleashed. A blade sailed silently at my head. I turned to admire its trajectory as I shifted to the side, catching it by the hilt and returning it to its owner in one smooth rotation.

Esti caught the rune-covered blade and narrowed her eyes at me.

"You've changed, vampire-lover," Esti said with a twisted smile. "You're faster."

"Upgrades," I said, and stepped toward her. "I'm going to kill you now."

Esti laughed, and waved me forward. "I was just getting started," she said, her voice almost a growl. "Come, dance."

She blocked my initial strike, a jab to her head, by slicing across with one of her blades. I materialized Ebonsoul and parried the next slash, and she laughed.

"You bitch," I said with a grunt as she shoved me back. Her strength was still something to be reckoned with.

"I'm going to enjoy eviscerating you," she said, lunging several times. "Your new power won't help you. You're still too slow, too weak, and you're too late to save your vampire. I'm going to break you both until you beg me to kill you."

"You're going to regret touching those close to me," I said, moving faster.

She deflected the first strike and slid back. I turned Ebonsoul and stopped one of her blades with the dull side as she closed in. I couldn't risk cutting her with a siphon. I followed up with a fist to her face, which she avoided, slamming an elbow into my side.

"Too slow, Strong," she said with a laugh as she backflipped away. "You move like you're standing still."

I let more power flow through me.

She slid forward and unleashed a barrage of slashes and strikes. I parried them, backpedaling at first, trying to keep up. My jacket quickly became shredded wheat under the onslaught. The only thing that stopped her was the Daystrider armor.

I unleashed even more power—and attacked.

She lunged again, stabbing forward with a blade aimed at my

eye. I ducked and released an uppercut into her arm, shattering it. She grunted in pain and attacked with her other arm. I moved to the side and looked as she moved in slow motion.

I trapped her arm against my body and slammed my forearm into her locked elbow, slamming the joint way past the point of extension. Her arm bent the wrong way, and then she screamed. She dropped her blades and lashed out with a kick. I saw the tip of the blade embedded in her boot and dodged back out of the way.

Her pain tolerance was impressive, but I needed to end this now. I focused my energy and quietly unleashed the word that came to me: *Uanescere*-disintegrate. A black orb formed in my hand, and I heard Monty yell in the distance.

"Simon! No!"

I turned to look at him as he moved toward me in slow motion. The rage in my chest broke free as I thought about what Esti had done—taking Peaches, torturing Chi, trying to repeatedly kill Monty and me. No one was safe around me as long as she lived. I knew she wouldn't stop. As long as she was alive, she would keep coming. I needed to stop her now.

I turned to face her, and for the first time saw an expression of fear on her face. It felt good. Black energy crackled around my arm as my heart filled with rage and a desire for vengeance.

"Time to die," I said, releasing the orb aiming for her chest. "Goodbye, bitch."

The black orb launched from my hand with a jolt of energy and raced at Esti. Her limp arms hung by her side and she knew, in that moment...this was the end. She closed her eyes just as a white orb of energy crashed into her side. The black orb slammed into her shoulder. Esti screamed as black energy traveled down her arm, removing it entirely.

"What...are you doing?" I asked, turning slowly towards Monty. "She's a threat. She needs to be eliminated."

Monty held up his hands and stood in front of me.

"Not like this, Simon," he said. "This isn't you."

I looked past him at the groaning Esti, who lay against the wall.

"I'll be right with you," I said, holding up a finger. "Give me a second."

"Fuck...fuck you, Strong."

"You took Peaches, and hurt Chi," I said, looking into her eyes. "I'm going to make you hurt."

"Stop this, Simon."

"Get out of my way, Monty."

"No. This isn't the way. This isn't you. You're not a murderer."

"She tried to kill Peaches, she tortured Chi, and she wants to kill me!"

"But, she hasn't succeeded," Monty said, still standing in my way. "You said so yourself, you can sense Peaches. He's not far. As for your vampire"—he pointed to where Chi lay on the ground —"she's still here. Don't do this."

The rage inside me wanted retribution.

"Get...out...of... my...way, Tristan." I formed another black orb.

"You are going to have to kill me first, Simon," Monty said, his voice hard. "This is wrong. You know this is wrong."

I froze. Everything inside me howled to destroy Esti, no matter who or what stood in my way. I was tired of being powerless; tired of having creatures and beings after me, threatening my life and the lives of those close to me. I was just tired of it all. I needed to end the threat.

I unleashed all of the power inside me into the orb. It tripled in size, as red and violet arcs of energy crackled around my body. Monty extended his arms and blocked my path.

The power inside me wanted to explode outward, devour everything in its path. I extended my arm upward and screamed as the energy raced out of my body, through the roof of the castle, and into the night sky.

I fell to my knees, completely spent. I looked over where Esti lay, eyes closed, groaning in pain, cowering as she held her injured side with her one remaining arm. Chi lay on the floor unconscious, tendrils gone, her body battered and beaten. The rage left me as I looked back at Monty. He nodded.

"It's over," he said, gesturing. "She won't attack us again. You made sure of that."

"You...you were right," I said as golden runes cascaded over my body.

That was the last thing I said before introducing my face to the floor and losing consciousness.

FORTY-TWO

A wet, slimy rag hit me across the face.

I opened my eyes to see an enormous pink tongue preparing to assault me.

"Agh! Stop," I said, trying to dodge the onslaught of slobber. "I'm awake...I'm awake."

<Again. My saliva has saved you. I think that deserves extra meat.>

I looked at my enormous hellhound and hugged his head, bringing him close.

<I thought I lost you, boy.>

<You can never lose me. We are bondmates.>

<They took you. I didn't know where you were, and I couldn't speak to you. Wait—how are you here?>

<The angry man and the scary lady found me. They made me delicious meat, which I ate. Now, I'm hungry.>

I looked around the room. I was still in Black Blossom, from the looks of things. Early morning light crept in through the window. I looked outside and noticed the cherry blossom trees planted all around the property. Belatedly, I realized the name referred to the cherries, not the blossoms.

I sat up with a groan. My body had mostly recovered, but I

ached everywhere. I let my senses expand, feeling for the power of the dragon's blood, but it was gone; or at the very least, I couldn't access it.

"You know what?" I said, rubbing Peaches' massive head and slowly swinging my legs out of bed. "I could use some coffee."

<Coffee is not meat. If you ate more meat, you wouldn't need my saliva so much. Meat makes you strong.>

<Yes, I know: meat is life.>

I made my way down to the kitchen, without running into anyone. I followed the aroma of coffee goodness and knew Monty had to be around somewhere—only he would have coffee brewing alongside a kettle of water.

I poured myself a small cup of inky goodness and stepped outside into the zen garden. Peaches padded next to me, close, in protective mode.

<I missed you.>

I looked down at him and realized my vulnerabilities were also my strengths. I rubbed his head.

<I missed you too, boy.>

"You've decided to rejoin us," Monty said from behind me. "Welcome back."

"Thanks," I said, turning. "I feel like warmed-over sh—"

He wasn't alone.

I realized I wasn't fully recovered when I saw the Blood Hunters. I hadn't sensed them. Either I was still out of it from the dragon's blood, or they were masters at energy camouflage. I'd like to think it was a bit of both.

A tall woman, dressed in Blood Hunter armor, stood next to Monty. She looked familiar…then I made the connection. She must have been related to Anastasia. My expression must have shifted, because she raised a hand.

"We are here to talk," she said with a slight accent tingeing her words.

"Who are you?"

"I am Valentina Mikaela Santiago, the current leader of the *Cazadoras de Sangre*—the Blood Hunters."

"I thought Esti—?"

"Estilete has engaged in unsanctioned operations and has been rogue since my cousin Anastasia's death."

Well, shit, this had gone south in a heartbeat. I was dressed in a robe, pulling off my best impression of Dex. The only weapon I had access to was Ebonsoul. It was time to try diplomacy.

"She tried to kill Chi."

"This Chi is a vampire, yes?"

"Yes."

"Killing vampires is what Blood Hunters do."

"She also kidnapped my hellhound and tried to erase me a few times."

"Yet, you and your hellhound still live."

"Yes."

"As well as the vampire she tried to eliminate, yes?"

"Yes," I said. "I can't give you back the blade. Not that I don't want to—I can't."

"Not while you live," Valentina said with a small smile, "you can't."

"Exactly."

"I can't give you Estilete," Valentina continued. "She is one of ours. She was wrong and will be punished severely for her actions—but she is still one of ours. Much like Anastasia was."

She was letting me know that she knew who killed her cousin.

"I can't give you Chi, either."

If Chi heard me speaking about her like property, she'd probably skewer me with Ebonsoul, after ripping it out of me first. Valentina flexed her jaw.

"Michiko Nakatomi is only a target because she is our sworn enemy—a vampire. You, however, are different."

"Different? How?"

"You, Simon Strong, killed Anastasia Santiago, leader of the Blood Hunters, and committed the high crime of bonding to a blood blade. What do you offer as recompense for your transgressions? What will you sacrifice?"

Monty stared hard at me and gave me the 'don't piss off the new leader of the Blood Hunters who came here with an army' stare. I thought about it for a moment and refrained from giving her my first answer, which would've resulted in much blood being spilled—mostly mine.

I also realized that, even though I ended Anastasia in battle while she was trying to kill those closest to me, actions had consequences.

"The only thing I can give you is...myself."

Valentina stared hard at me in silence.

"Very well," she said after a few more seconds of giving me the once over. "I speak for every Blood Hunter when I say your sacrifice is worthy. In time, we will need you to honor your word."

She flexed her wrist and materialized a blade, causing me to tense up reflexively. She ran it gently across her palm cutting her hand, then extended it to me. I looked down at the plain weapon; it was missing the runes most Blood Hunter blades carry. The last time I did something like this I nearly died. With a deep breath, I took the offered blade, cut my hand and clasped hers.

"And if I refuse to honor my word?" I asked. These were Blood Hunters I was dealing with, after all.

"This is a blood oath. If you break this pact, everything and everyone you love and hold dear will be stripped from you and destroyed. This, I promise."

"I understand," I said, removing my hand slowly enough to let her see that the wound was already gone. Valentina raised an eyebrow in surprise, but quickly hid it.

"I will make a promise of my own," I said. "If any Blood Hunter touches anyone under my protection, vampire or otherwise, I will make it my personal mission to erase your order from the face of the earth, as long as I live."

Valentina held my gaze and stared. I stared back. Combined, we had at least a five on the glare-o-meter with an extra dose of Eastwood on both our parts.

"We are in agreement," she said. "We will speak soon, Chosen of Kali."

They turned and left. When they were gone, I breathed a sigh of relief. Monty escorted them off the property, and I found a bench in the quiet zen garden. The sun still hadn't completely risen, and I contemplated the stones. Peaches sat next to me and sprawled. A few seconds later, a soft snore escaped him.

"You didn't have to come after me," a voice said from behind me. "That was foolish and nearly cost you your life."

It was Chi.

I didn't turn around.

"You need to be running the Dark Council. Your brother is worried."

"I tried to push you away, and then you went and started a small war."

"I'm funny that way," I said. "Why did you leave?"

"Dealing with the threat of Esti and the factions in the Council would have put too many people in danger," she answered. "People I care about. I knew she wanted me. I wanted to choose the battleground."

"So, you came home," I said, looking around the property. "I like it. It's quiet and peaceful."

She sat next to me on the bench.

"Quiet, yes. Peaceful? Not for me."

"The threats?" I asked. "Euthanizing Peaches and erasing Monty?"

"Empty. Achieving either would be a near impossible task."

I nodded my head.

"Are you going back to the Council? Ken seems to think it's the best place for you."

"What do you think?"

"I think the Council needs a strong leader, and you've been the strongest so far."

"Agreed," she said. "For now, it is my *on*—my obligation—and I will fulfill it."

"We need to get back, too," I said. "Will I see you when we get back?"

"*Koi no yokan*," she said, standing.

"What is that?"

"A concept I am learning to embrace," she said. "I'm certain we will see each other soon. In the meantime, I wish you luck in dealing with that."

"With what?" I turned to see Monty approaching me with Fumiko and the bankermages in tow. When I turned back, Chi had Batmanned me and vanished.

"Mr. Strong, I hope you are aware that the destruction of an ancient edifice is a punishable offense in Japan," Fumiko started. "I don't know or care what you do back in your country, but here, we respect our history."

Three of the bankermages surrounded me. Monty stood back, crossed his arms and shook his head.

"The travesty," Monty said as I stared at him. "Some of these structures are priceless. This is a living part of the country's history, Simon."

"I'm not a mage," I said, looking at Monty, pleading. "Tell them."

"Don't lie to me, Mr. Strong," Fumiko answered. "The energy signature around the destruction matches yours. If you would come with us, please?"

I got up and considered, just for a second, letting Peaches loose on them.

"Go with them," Monty said, suppressing a smile. "I will have it resolved by the time they get to Osaka."

"I'm so glad this is entertaining to you," I said as the bankermages escorted me into the castle. I glared at them. "Are you three going to dress me, too?"

"No need," Fumiko said. "We have a change of clothing for you in the van. Let's go."

"You may want to leave your creature with me," Monty said. "No need to create an incident. If you're going to be busy, perhaps your creature and I can visit some of the more interesting sights. Do you know how long he will be detained, Ms. Ishikawa?"

"As long as necessary," Fumiko said. "We take destruction of property seriously here, Mr. Strong."

"Oh, hilarious," I said, leaving the zen garden. I knew whose tea was going to get spiked with Deathwish when we got back. "You better fix this."

"If only you had more control of your abilities," Monty yelled after me as the van pulled away. "I'll see you in Osaka!"

FORTY-THREE

The Randy Rump—NYC.

I sat in the corner of the Randy Rump as the sun was just coming over the horizon. Peaches was doing his usual sprawl by my feet, after devouring several pounds of prime pastrami.

Monty eventually got all of the charges dropped. He took his sweet time, and I think he really did go sight-seeing with Peaches, which must have scared most of the population.

The castle was repaired and Chi waived any fines for the damage caused. Dex ended up repairing the damage to the castle after he and TK gave me a thorough runic examination.

Apparently, the dragon's blood was still present in my system, but any power I possessed because of it, had gone dormant. I admit I missed having access to the power, although I didn't miss how I had almost blasted Monty when the rage took over.

I heard the door to the Randy Rump open, and looked up. Being a designated neutral zone, the place was never completely dead, but it was usually empty at this hour.

A second later, everything became hazy and out of focus. Time had stopped. I looked down to make sure I hadn't accidentally pressed my mark. A thin man, dressed in blue jeans and a white dress shirt, stood in the doorway.

He gazed around the shop until we locked eyes. He smiled with a nod and walked over. I didn't know who he was, but I didn't sense any harmful intent. I looked down at Peaches, who kept snoring by my feet.

It was clear, he wasn't frozen.

"Mind if I sit?" the man asked, pulling out a chair opposite me. "I won't be long."

I motioned with my hand as I took another sip of coffee. Monty would be along soon. It seemed Ezra had an emergency only we could handle.

"I'm waiting for someone, but go ahead."

"I know," the man said, and my defenses kicked up a notch.

"Excuse me? Who are you?"

"Terribly sorry, where are my manners?" he extended a hand. "Sidney Rat, Lead Designer. My friends call me Sid."

"Sid Rat? Designer? What do you design?"

"Streams, specifically time streams."

"I think you have me confused with someone else."

"You're Simon, right?" Sid asked. "Simon Strong?"

"I'm sorry, do I know you?"

"Not yet, you don't. I won't take up much of your time. Just need to give you this."

He slid a keepsaker box across the table, and my defenses kicked into high gear. "Last time I dealt with one of those, it was bad," I said, eyeing the box warily. "What is it?"

Sid let a finger fall on the top of the box.

"This...this is purpose. This is a ripple in the pond."

"A what?"

Time snapped back, and Sid was gone. I looked down at the box as Monty entered the Rump.

"Ezra's waiting," Monty said, coming to my table. "It sounds dire. Are you ready?"

"It's always dire," I said, grabbing the box, putting it in a pocket and standing, coffee in hand. "Let's go. I'm driving."

"I don't know if I'd call what you do 'driving,'" he said, turning to Jim and waving. "One to go, please. Is your creature joining us?"

"Of course he is," I said, heading out of the Rump. "Let's go, boy."

I opened the rear suicide door, and Peaches slid into the Dark Goat, tipping it to one side. Monty closed the door and jumped in.

"Another day, another crisis."

I tossed Monty the keepsaker.

"What's this?" he asked, looking at the box. "Where did you get this?"

"You ever hear of the Designers?"

"Can't say that I have, no."

"Maybe we need to pay Professor Ziller a visit."

"As soon as we see what has Ezra agitated," Monty answered. "I'd prefer to keep him calm."

"Sounds like a plan. It's a good day to meet Death."

I turned the engine on, and the Dark Goat roared before settling into a throaty rumble.

"Try not to crush anything on the way there," Monty said, gesturing around the box. "It's locked tight."

"I think I know who has the key."

I floored the gas and sped downtown.

THE END

AUTHOR NOTES

Thank you for reading this story and jumping back into the

world of Monty & Strong.

Writing this story was a blast, even though it was a little light on Peaches, for that I extend my most heartfelt apologies. Like you, I always love seeing Peaches in action, this book needed to show Simon what it means to be vulnerable—in more ways than one.

It was great being able to (virtually) visit Japan. Amazingly, much of it was left intact, they didn't even set off Mt. Fuji... incredible. I wouldn't want MS&P to get blamed for more destruction overseas, they're still dealing with London backlash. Many readers felt that Esti didn't get what she deserved...pain, followed by more pain, followed by extermination. I feel your anguish. All I can say is—this isn't the last time you see Esti.

It was requested that I explain the last statement Chi makes(*koi no yokan*). I felt it was best left untranslated, but please feel free to look it up. More on that will develop in future books. Try not not to dislike her too much—everything has a reason and everything is connected.

With each book, I want to introduce you to different elements of the world Monty & Strong inhabit, slowly revealing who they are and why they make the choices they do. Many times you will feel like Simon, a little out of depth. That's intentional, because we've all had experiences where we didn't know what was going on. Simon lives that everyday. He deals with it by being a smart ass and occasionally speaking before he thinks. If you want to know how they met, that story is in **NO GOD IS SAFE**, which is a short, explaining how Tristan and Simon worked their first case.

There are some references you will understand and some... you may not. This may be attributable to my age (I'm older than Monty, or feel that way most mornings) or to my love of all things sci-fi and fantasy. As a reader, I've always enjoyed finding these "Easter Eggs" in the books I read. I hope you do too. These references occur spontaneously(Chapter 34...again)and I barely have control of where they will pop up. If there is a reference you don't get, feel free to email me and I will explain it...maybe. Bribing with coffee and chocolate has been known to work wonders.

You will notice that Simon is still a smart-ass (deserving a large head smack) snark, and many times, he's clueless about what's going on. He's also acquired, in addition to more spells (an anemic magic missile and deathane sausage), dragonblood. What will happen when he tries using magic will be hilarious and dangerous. There is more of that to come in the next books. He still needs tons of practice and maybe a basement of his own to blow up.

Simon is slowly wrapping his head around the world of magic, but it's a vast universe and he has no map. Bear with him —he's still new to the immortal, magical world he's been delicately shoved into. Fortunately, he has Monty, Peaches, Dex, LD, TK, and Chi to nudge (or blast) him in the right direction. Each book will reveal more about their backgrounds and lives before they met. Rather than hit you with a whole history, I want you to learn about them slowly, the way we do with a person we just met—over time (and many large cups of Deathwish Coffee).

Thank you for taking the time to read this book. I wrote it for you and I hope you enjoyed spending a few more hours getting in (and out of) trouble with the Trio of Terror. If you really enjoyed this story, I need you to do me a HUGE favor— **Please leave a review**. It's really important and helps the book (and me). Plus, it means Peaches gets new reinforced titanium alloy chew toys, besides my arms, legs, and assorted furniture to shred. And I get to keep him at normal size (most of the time). He's also thinking of getting Rags some toys and we have to help him impress her. She has very high standards and only the best will do.

We want to help Peaches, don't we?

SPECIAL MENTIONS

Larry & Tammy-WOUF: Because you are ever present.

Tammy: because some things are Nanatacular and if not they are certainly Dexciting!

Tammy: because no one really wants to ride the lightning. Tomorrow is never here, after all.

Tammy: because TK is the bogeyman's bogeyman.

Tammy: that magic-imbued slap of healing because stupidity should hurt.

Tammy: because zillerfrying is much more intense than zillerfying

Marc & Gemma: For places Monty & Simon can visit...and destroy.

The M&S Effect is just like the Butterfly Effect, but with destruction.

Marc: there's no truth to the rumor that the latin means: "Where we go destruction follows."

Marc: for suggesting the recap be done by Peaches.

Dan: for Tropical Fruit Bubbilicious, and by default, Hubba Bubba and Skittles...see what you started?

Beth: remember *investigate* is just another word for *demolish*.

Chris: for dance of the Mage...everybody dies.

Earl: for the Dark Goat's color...infrablack is perfect.

Kirsten BW: for quanked...challenge accepted!

Anthony: for the Emergency DGAS Attack LMAO...those things can be deadly!

Dolly: for *koi no yokan* to describe Simon and Chi.

Orlando A. Sanchez
www.orlandoasanchez.com

Orlando has been writing ever since his teens when he was immersed in creating scenarios for playing Dungeon and Dragons with his friends every weekend. The worlds of his books are urban settings with a twist of the paranormal lurking just behind the scenes and generous doses of magic, martial arts, and mayhem. He currently resides in Queens, NY with his wife and children and can often be found lurking in the local coffee shops where most of his writing is done.

BITTEN PEACHES PUBLISHING

Thanks for Reading

If you enjoyed this book, would you please **leave a review** at the site you purchased it from? It doesn't have to be long... just a line or two would be fantastic and it would really help me out.

Bitten Peaches Publishing offers more books by this author. From science fiction & fantasy to adventure & mystery, we bring the best stories for adults and kids alike.

www.BittenPeachesPublishing.com

More books by Orlando A. Sanchez

The Warriors of the Way
The Karashihan*•The Spiritual Warriors•The Ascendants•The Fallen Warrior•The Warrior Ascendant•TheMaster Warrior

John Kane
The Deepest Cut*•Blur

Sepia Blue
The Last Dance*•Rise of the Night•Sisters•Nightmare

Chronicles of the Modern Mystics
The Dark Flame•A Dream of Ashes

Montague & Strong Detective Agency Novels
Tombyards & Butterflies•Full Moon Howl•Blood is
Thicker•Silver Clouds Dirty Sky•Homecoming•Dragons &
Demigods•Bullets & Blades•Hell Hath No Fury•Reaping Wind

Montague & Strong Detective Agency Stories
No God is Safe•The Date•The War Mage•A Proper Hellhound

Brew & Chew Adventures
Hellhound Blues

Night Warden Novels
Wander•ShadowStrut

Division 13
The Operative•The Magekiller

Blackjack Chronicles
The Dread Warlock

The Assassins Apprentice
The Birth of Death

*Books denoted with an asterisk are **FREE** via my website
—www.orlandoasanchez.com

ACKNOWLEDEGEMENTS

With each book, I realize that every time I learn something about this craft, it highlights so many things I still have to learn. Each book, each creative expression, has a large group of people behind it.

This book is no different.

Even though you see one name on the cover, it is with the knowledge that I am standing on the shoulders of the literary giants that informed my youth and am supported by my generous readers who give of their time to jump into the adventures of my overactive imagination.

I would like to take a moment to express my most sincere thanks:

To my Tribe: You are the reason I have stories to tell. You cannot possibly fathom how much and how deeply I love you all.

To Lee: Because you were the first audience I ever had. I love you, sis.

To the Logsdon Family: The words, *thank you* are insufficient to describe the gratitude in my heart for each of you. JL, your support always demands I bring my best, my A-game, and produce the best story I can. You, Lorelei(my Uber Jeditor) and now Audrey(my new Uber Editor), are the reason I am where I am today. Thank you for the notes, challenges, corrections, advice, and laughter. Your patience is truly infinite. *Arigatogozaimasu.*

To The Montague & Strong Case Files Group—AKA The MoB (Mages of Badassery): When I wrote T&B, there were fifty-five members in The MoB. As of this release there are over one-thousand members in the MoB. I am honored to be able to call you my MoB Family. Thank you for being part of this group and M&S. You make this possible. **THANK YOU.**

To the WTA—The Incorrigibles: JL, Ben Z., Eric QK., and S.S.
They sound like a bunch of badass misfits, because they are. My exposure to the deranged and deviant brain trust you all represent helped me be the author I am today. I have officially gone to the *dark side* thanks to all of you. I humbly give you my thanks, and…it's all your fault.

To The English Advisory: Aaron, Penny, Carrie and all of the UK MoB. For all things English…thank you.

To DEATH WISH COFFEE: This book (and every book I write) has been fueled by generous amounts of the only coffee on the planet (and in space) strong enough to power my very twisted imagination. Is there any other coffee that can compare? I think not. DEATH WISH-thank you!

To Deranged Doctor Design: Kim, Darja, Tanja, and Milo.
If you've seen the covers of my books and been amazed, you can thank the very talented and gifted creative team at DDD.

They take the rough ideas I give them, and produce incredible covers that continue to surprise and amaze me. Each time, I find myself striving to write a story worthy of the covers they produce. DDD, you embody professionalism and creativity. Thank you for the great service and spectacular covers. **YOU GUYS RULE!**

To you, the reader: I was always taught to save the best for last. I write these stories for you. Thank you for jumping down the rabbit holes of *what if?* with me. You are the reason I write the stories I do. You keep reading...I'll keep writing. Thank you for your support and encouragement.

CONTACT ME

I really do appreciate your feedback. You can let me know what you thought of the story by emailing me at:

www.orlando@orlandoasanchez.com

To get **FREE** stories, please visit my page at:
www.orlandoasanchez.com

For more information on Monty, Strong, Peaches, and the Orlandoverse of characters…come join the MoB Family on Facebook!
You can find us at:
Montague & Strong Case Files

If you enjoyed the book, please leave a review! They really help the book and help other readers find good stories to read. **THANK YOU!**

ART SHREDDERS

No book is the work of one person. I am fortunate enough to have an amazing team of advance readers and shredders. They give their time and keen eyes to provide notes, insight, and corrections (dealing wonderfully with my dreaded comma allergy). They help make every book and story go from good to great. Each and every one of you helped make this book fantastic.

THANK YOU

ART SHREDDERS

Alisia S. Amy R. Anne M. Audra V. M. Audrey C. Barbara H. Bennah P. Bethany S. Beverly C. Brett W. Cam S. Carrie Anne O. Cassandra H. Cat. Chris C II. Claudia L-S. Colleen T. Dana A. Daniel P. Darren M. Davina N. Dawn McQ. M. Denise K. Diana G. Diane K. Dolly S. Donna Y H. Dorothy MPG. Elizabeth. Hal B. Helen D. Jeem. Jen C. Jennifer H. Joscelyn S. Julie P. Justin B. Karen H. Karen H. Larry Diaz T. Laura Cadger R. Laura T. Lesley S. LZ. Malcolm R. Mary Anne P. MaryAnn S. Maryelaine E-F. Melody DeL. Mike H. Missy B. Natalie F. Nick C. Patricia O'N.

Penny C-M. RC B. Rene C. Rob H. Sara Mason B. Shanon O.B.
Sharon H. Shawnie N. Stacey S. Stephanie C. Stephen B. Sue W.
Susie J. Tami C. Tammy Ashwin K. Tammy T. Tanya A. Ted C.
Tehrene H. Terri A. Tom D. Tommy O. Tracey M.C. Wanda C-J.
Wendy S. Zak K.

Thanks for Reading

If you enjoyed this book, would you please leave a review at the site you purchased it from? It doesn't have to be a book report... just a line or two would be fantastic and it would really help us out!

CPSIA information can be obtained
at www.ICGtesting.com
Printed in the USA
LVHW040210291019
635549LV00003B/820